THE ROAD TO ZARAUZ

Sam Adams

Parthian, Cardigan SA43 1ED
www.parthianbooks.com
First published in 2020
© Sam Adams 2020
ISBN 978-1-912681-85-3 paperback
ISBN 978-1-912681-89-1 ebook
Edited by Richard Davies
Cover design Emily Courdelle
Typeset by Elaine Sharples
Printed by 4Edge Limited
Published with the financial support of the Books Council of Wales
British Library Cataloguing in Publication Data
A cataloguing record for this book is available from the British Library.

To Muriel

'If I were pressed to say why I loved him, I could only shrug – because it was him; because it was me.'

Michel Eyquem de Montaigne

The Perseids brought it all out of the past, with the force of a blow that leaves you winded. The night lurched and swooped suddenly down. The boy lay still, stretched out on his back, but when I sat up, gasping, I glimpsed the pale disc of his face as he turned to see what had startled me.

'It's all right,' I said, though it wasn't. 'Anything yet?'

Just then a brief, bright streak fell across the inky sky, followed by three more.

'There, there,' he said, pointing. 'Did you see them?'

Was it the brilliance and brevity of that streak across the sky that brought Richie at once and with such clarity to my mind? No, that would have been a spontaneous imaginative leap I am incapable of, though I have thought of it since – a symbol of a short life – a cliché. It was the sky alone, the black starry sky, that jolted the memory.

Earlier that August day, with the weather forecast to be warm and cloudless after dark, the newspaper had promised the Perseid shower would be a rare spectacle. We talked about it over breakfast. The boy said he had never seen a falling star and this seemed an opportunity too good to miss. His parents didn't think much of the idea, but to have a ten-year-old interested in a natural phenomenon rather than a computer game I thought worth encouraging. 'I'll keep him company,' I said. My grandson and I had done little enough together, for he was growing up three hundred miles away, and my daughter and her husband had busy lives; their visits were infrequent and brief.

Only a few minutes had passed since we closed the back door behind us, found our way by torchlight down the garden steps and across the sloping grass, already damp with dew, beyond the two apple trees. It was ten o'clock, his bedtime as his mother pointed out, when we spread the old tartan travelling rug and settled ourselves down. Once the torch was switched off, despite the chain of street lamps along the road the other side of the house, there were stars enough to be seen, though the moon was down.

Fully sixty years had passed since I had lain in the open looking up into the night. That was the trigger. Then it had been an unsullied, perfect black filled with stars of astonishing brilliancy. In all my life before I had never seen such scintillation, so many pulsing, glittering specks, and as I turned my head slowly left then right, a long, bright cloud, a shimmering river of light, running across the western sky. I remember thinking that is what's meant by unearthly beauty, colourless, silent, alien, and the shock of hearing Richie sobbing. I was then not quite twice the age of my grandson and in some respects less sophisticated than he already was. On that holiday, through hot weeks at the height of summer, we lay in the open on other nights full of stars, but none held quite the fascination and existential unease of that first one. Where were we that night, all those years ago? Was it the far south of France? Or over the border in Spain?

It had been so long, so many years, since the time when thoughts of that holiday tormented me like a fever day and night. You cannot will yourself to forget a painful memory, nor can you easily conceal it from yourself beneath layers of mundane affairs and events, but like the murdered corpse, it will rise bloated to the surface of the lake, or in bony fragments jut from the shallow grave. Silting over took a long time. I might have thought I was somehow 'cured' of it, or inured to it, when I could shake my head and turn my attention to other things. At last, mercifully, I didn't think of it at all, until that night, when it returned with a rush and left me distracted and stammering, so that the boy and his father looked at me curiously.

'Are you all right, Dad?'

'Yes, of course.' I was irritated by my daughter's concern.

As the boy was hurried to bed ('It's an early start tomorrow!'), I took my usual chair to watch *Newsnight*. But I couldn't settle, couldn't get into the programme at all.

'I think that's enough for me,' I said. 'I remember when you used to get pleasant news occasionally. I'll say goodnight.' I bent to kiss my daughter's cheek, sorry for my shortness earlier.

I wouldn't say I am a good sleeper – average I suppose for someone my age, but that night I lay awake for hours, thinking over the journey, long ago, through France and Spain, trying to piece it all together. If I slept at all I am sure in my dreams, too, I was there on the road, the road to Zarauz. When the alarm went I was glad to get up, fearful that what had long been unthought of had returned, and some of the images, the voices, the words even, as sharp as a goad.

As soon as my daughter and her family had left after breakfast, I couldn't rest until I had started looking for the few sad souvenirs of August 1954. I knew what I was seeking, and where it probably was. I have always had difficulty in throwing stuff away. It's a common enough failing. Unwanted things worm to the back of drawers, or the far dark corners of cupboards, and perchance disturbed in those resting places are put into cardboard boxes and lugged up to the loft, where they can linger a lifetime and more, for one's children, or strangers even, to come upon, ponder over briefly and throw out or burn. I lowered the loft ladder took the torch and clambered up to look.

Though still morning, it was already oppressively hot in the low, upturned V of the space under the roof. There was no electricity and no skylight. The torch played on rafters and felting above as I rose to the lip of the opening and, when I had hoisted myself in, lit the yellow, hairy insulation thick between the beams where I trod carefully. The boxes, six or seven of varying sizes, lay inconveniently close to the eaves, so that I had to balance on a beam bent double, my throat full of clogging dust, to reach them. Black dust coated everything, shimmering faintly as I swung the torchlight over the boxes. I was lucky, for the third I opened with gritty fingers contained a collection of vintage rugby match programmes and the object I was looking for – an empty Player's Medium Cut cigarette pack of fifty. A few moments more and I was taking deep breaths of fresher air on the landing, the ladder back in place and loft door closed.

Richie, Alan and Gwyn had shared the cost of the cigarettes at the duty-free shop on the cross-channel ferry. As a non-smoker I had been glad to be spared the expense. A dark blue cardboard box of fifty Player's, about nine inches by six, with the familiar trademark in the top right-hand corner, the bust of a bearded sailor encircled by a whitish, rope-wrapped lifebelt. It had survived the journey well, and the years that followed. The silver-foil lining was intact too, and when I pulled open the overlapping sheet, there were those few souvenirs of our holiday, which, despite everything that happened, I had preserved by putting them away from me: the postcards I sent home from France and Spain, one smudged with a dribble of wine, and the photographs, ten of them, black and white, and small, about two inches square. They were taken with the Brownie box camera my older sister had pressed on me.

She must have had them printed when she wanted to put a fresh reel of film in the camera. At the time I couldn't bear to look at them, but neither could I destroy them. Yes, I put them away with the postcards my mother had kept, the entire record of those weeks, apart from what long suppressed memory had refused to erase.

The photos are of places on the route – a richly carved church or cathedral facade, which I feel certain is Orleans, and landscapes that caught my eye. The great overhanging cliff with the car a mere dot on the winding road at its foot must be somewhere in the Pyrénées. The one of Alan pointing to a broken viaduct among rocky peaks surely means something. Perhaps he was telling us it was hit by bombs or artillery during the Spanish Civil War, which had ended only fifteen years before and had left its mark. Alan knew about such things. In 1954, we were among the very small number of travellers moving around Spain under Franco's dictatorship and, beneath a show of bravado, rather wary on that account.

Even when I peer through a magnifying glass the faces in most of the photos remain indistinct. One Alan must have taken has Richie, Gwyn and me leaning on a sign saying 'Madrid' in large white letters on a dark background. This was the apex of our journey south. Beyond the sign, a row of low trees stretches out along a straggling grassy verge, each slim trunk painted with a broad white band, an aid to after-dark traffic no doubt, but it's day and the road is empty apart from our car. A matching pair of brutal, new three-storey buildings march down the opposite side of the road. Each is pierced with three identical rows of windows, squarish but with a low arch at the top, and apparently unglazed. Goodness knows who the rooms they lit were meant to accommodate, office workers perhaps (without balconies, without a place for airing clothes, surely not families). Then again they suggest nothing so much as barracks for the military, and appear uninhabited, probably unfinished. There we were, in August 1954, at the side of a broad road in some suburb of a great city of which I have not the faintest memory. We rarely lingered in towns, where prices were prohibitive for our shallow pockets, and presumably Madrid fell under the general ban.

Gwyn and Richie, I remember, came from different sides of the same south Wales valley. They had attended the same grammar school and both had fallen under the influence of a charismatic young history teacher. Her enthusiasm for the subject had made them apply for the university course she had graduated from not long before. Otherwise they had little in common. Gwyn, with fairish, wavy hair, and a square, bland face, was quiet and stolid, wary of uncertainty, while Richie's lean and angular features beneath straight dark hair swept in a wing across his forehead shone with brightness. He was quick and decisive. In class discussion he was always first to answer a question or offer an opinion. It didn't seem to matter that he was sometimes wildly wrong. I remember thinking he must be what they call 'mercurial'. Looking back, I believe I should have seen in him a congenital risk-taker, a flirter with fate. Within a couple of weeks of going up to university, he had done nothing to find accommodation, but a chance encounter with Gwyn solved that problem. Gwyn was fixed up in digs recommended by his chapel minister, who knew the landlady. Keen to have at least one familiar face in a new environment, 'Why don't you join me?' he said. Even at that late stage, there was still a room available, and when they got there Richie began to understand why. They found themselves on a newish estate some distance from college, which meant a bus ride to lectures. At the beginning of the second term, Gwyn brought his bicycle up on the train to avoid hanging around for buses. Richie didn't have a bicycle, but from time to time persuaded Gwyn to lend his. Gwyn had fallen for the landlady's daughter, Evelyn, a tall, fair, pallid girl, who was just out of school. Richie told me she was looking for shop work in town, and Gwyn was content to hang around digs when nothing demanded his presence elsewhere. He had even been thinking of looking for a summer job somewhere near coll. so that their romance could continue, perhaps blossom, over the warm months. In the end, it was she, Evelyn, who persuaded him to go with us, perhaps as a test. If he returned unsullied from foreign shores, then she was his, fairly won. Or was it a test of her own resolve? She was barely out of girlhood, had not tried such powers as she possessed on other boys. The separation gave both for a while an open field, a proving ground for him and her.

Anyway, the bike would be there, idle, and Gwyn occasionally lent it to Richie, but didn't wait to see him speeding down the hill, bespectacled, dark hair swept back by the wind, and hands ostentatiously in his pockets.

I got to know Richie at the beginning of the year. After lectures he would be scrabbling in his pockets for a cigarette and matches, but once lit-up he was ready to talk. And what a talker he was: the usual stuff about pictures we had seen, who made a fool of himself at the hop on Saturday, the gang who played cards constantly in the college union lounge (Did they ever go to lectures?). But also about books. Mostly about books. 'I started reading *Tess* after supper,' I remember him saying, 'and I couldn't put it down. Read through the night. Tribulation piled on tribulation, relentlessly. Finished about half past four. God, I felt depressed.'

I was often no more than a good listener in these conversations, but I took a lot in and if I began to think about, properly *think* about, all the books there waiting on the library shelves, it was down to him rather than any lecturer.

He soon learned I didn't share his addiction to nicotine. It didn't matter to him, of course – or to me: I was used to being the only non-smoker at home. Back then, tobacco companies' advertisements projected an image of the smoker as elegant sophisticate. Richie was otherwise. He smoked feverishly in quick, strong pulls, the tip glowing brightly and the ash growing perceptibly at each drag. But he was a good talker, even with fag dangling, and that was what counted.

He and Gwyn didn't have much in common. Gwyn wasn't the bookish sort – studied no more than was necessary to keep up and pass exams, but his father had got on in the world. After leaving school at fourteen, he had attended evening classes in book-keeping and accountancy, so instead of working underground, as most did, he got a job in the colliery office, and made a career of it.

'As you'd expect, there were those in the Band Club back home who were sure strings had been pulled,' Richie said. 'Gwyn's grandfather, dead now, was a big man in the Labour party.' And slipping into the familiar rhythm and intonation of home, 'They got a car. You seen it?'

At that time, there were very few cars in valley streets. We used to play football in the road while we were waiting for the bus to take us back to school after dinner. What a change. Now you can hardly step off the pavement for parked cars. Well, Gwyn's father had a car, and wore a suit and clean shirt to work and, at the end of the week, stood behind the clerks handing out pay packets to the black-faced miners with gleaming white eyes and a block of wood under the arm for sticks to light the fire.

Gwyn was like his father, Richie said, a bit podgy, fleshy-faced, 'But he's all right. I got on well with him in school – get on well with him now.'

Before the trip, I knew Gwyn only slightly, by sight, and with the trip ending as it did, ours was not an acquaintance I was keen to keep up afterwards. Besides, he had Evelyn. Whatever leisure he had was devoted to her. He didn't hang around college, didn't go for coffees, or out drinking in the evenings. He got on his bike and pedalled back to digs, where, Richie used to say, 'He's got his feet under the table – all kinds of extras. Nothing too good for Gwyn.' You could tell even then that all he really wanted was to get married and settle down. He made an effort to join in while we were in France and Spain, did his bit as co-driver to give Alan a break, drank with us in bars, smoked his share of the rationed cigarettes, and lost some of his tentativeness and suspicion of strange places and people. He was beginning to be less inhibited, even to enjoy himself, by the time we reached Zarauz.

Alan alone knew where he was going, and we were glad to be led. There would have been no expedition to Spain if he had not proposed and planned it. Small and spare, with large eyes and a long, sensitive nose, he was the most kindly and undemonstrative of leaders, having no inclination or need to assert himself. We readily gave him the respect due to an elder with experience beyond our imagining. He had been a soldier, served in the war, whereas we had nothing to look back on but school and, by the time we began the expedition, a couple of years of uni behind us. In his late twenties, he had decided to study history at university, to understand better, he said, that part of it he had been involved in. He was determined to do well – and when the time came he did. Gwyn and Richie usually sat next to him in history classes and they soon became friends. Then Richie, suddenly ambitious to be a writer, opted for honours English, as I had done from the outset, and linked the four of us.

Although we were in the same honours class and straight from school, Richie was more than a year older, the result of some hiatus or setback at an earlier stage in his education. I never asked about it, but it made a difference. I recognised he was more adult in experience and taste, while I was still struggling out of adolescence. It made no difference to our friendship. Our common background helped: we both came from the mining valleys, his across a few mountains to the east of mine, but a good thirty miles by road. We arranged that I should visit him at home during the Easter vacation to decide finally whether we would join the trip to Spain, which we had discussed together, and Alan was determined on, whether Richie, Gwyn and I were in or out.

'Come to our place. We'll have a drink and you can stay overnight and go back the next morning.'

It seemed a good idea. 'Probably a Saturday would be best?' I said

'No – not Saturday. Mass Sunday morning.'

'I didn't know you were Catholic. You haven't mentioned going to mass in term.'

'There you have me. But then my mother isn't here. I was brought up in the faith. My Nan, my mother's mother, was Irish.'

Lectures over, early in the evening, we were sitting in the usual café, which was almost empty. I was wondering whether to go back to the library, Richie waiting for the next bus out to his digs. It had been a grey day of constant drizzle, and chill, not the faintest hint of spring. What he told me came as a surprise. I knew from early conversations with him he was an only child, and that he lived alone with his mother, his father having died when he was seven.

'He'd had this terrible pain in his side and been sick,

but went to work anyway,' he once told me. 'Couldn't afford not to. And he collapsed there. Burst appendix – peritonitis.'

I didn't know about his religion, and that he took it seriously, at least when he was home. I too had been a church-goer, initially at my mother's urging, though later I was drawn to regular attendance by the repeated patterns of the liturgy, the dramatic gestures and eloquence of our vicar, who made the most of his histrionic skills and, above all, the language of the King James Bible. Was this Richie's experience, I wondered.

He told me his first communion was when he was nearly eight, preceded by first confession. Of the confessional I knew nothing.

'It was the same for me; it's the same for everyone,' he said, 'before your first. I remember, although my mother had tried to explain why and how we confessed, and of course we had been prepared by the priest, it was still so very strange sitting there facing the grille, with the outline of Father Trevor's head the other side. My mother told me I should think about my sins before confession, but I couldn't. What had I done? Did I have bad thoughts? What were bad thoughts? Had I committed bad deeds? Was it bad that I'd peed in the ferns on the mountain? Everybody else did when they were taken short. Was it bad I had elbowed a girl in our class – it was our first year in junior school – when she pushed in front of me as we were queuing to go into the hall for dinners? I don't remember what I said in the end, but the priest said, "I absolve you from your sins in the name of the Father, the Son, and the Holy Spirit", so it was all right. It got easier as the months passed, and the years – a routine. Until I felt the prickings of lust. *Prickings,* that's the right word, isn't it? How old was I then? Twelve? I didn't know, still don't know, how to confess what I feel about girls. For ages I agonised over it. It was unfair to give me a body that reacted in that way at the thought alone of a girl's body. Such enthralling excitement of the senses. And if I yielded to the thrill ... let's not beat about the bush: if I wanked, did I have to have to confess it as a sin? What about the priest? Did he have the same urge? And give in to it? I used to sit in the confessional and after "Bless me father for I have sinned", I wouldn't know what to say, until Father Trevor, who surely sensed the chaos in my head, would prompt me, "Have you had impure thoughts, my son?" I used to sit there wondering. Which particular thoughts had been impure? And why were they *impure?* What sort of pollution was in my head, and almost omnipresent in my body? In the end I just used to say, "Yes, Father" and leave it at that. He didn't seem to mind. And I didn't think of it much of the time, but at those moments – you know, when you've put the book down, and are settling to sleep, and you have this erection ... well, you know.'

He peered at me over his glasses. I couldn't bring myself to say a word, but a vague nod and shrug was enough to set him off again.

'As a counterbalance to the weight of sin, when I was younger, I used to practise self-denial. Did you look forward to "Take It From Here!" on the wireless? I did. It was the best thing of the week, and I really wanted to hear it. But I thought I could build up credit in Heaven by not listening to it on Tuesday evening – used to catch the recording on Saturday morning instead. Stupid things like that. But at the time I believed they were helping to save my soul. And half of me still does believe. I *want* to believe.'

He bowed his head and massaged his forehead with the fingers of both hands, then looked up and sighed, half-smiling. 'Goodness knows what Father Trevor would have said if I'd told him all I was thinking and feeling.'

He paused while I sat silent, not knowing what to say or do.

'I'm not sure how I stand in God's judgement now. The lust is worse than ever, but I don't go to mass, not here anyway – no confession, no absolution.' And he laughed hopelessly.

'I'm a lapsed Anglican,' I said, trying to share his gloom, 'lower than that you cannot go. I'm beyond redemption, though the hymns still run around in my head and Bible verses rise up from somewhere in my memory. We're probably both stuck with guilt.'

'We've only one life here, nothing's surer, whatever happens or doesn't happen after. It's our choice what we do with it. Yes, there are circumstances that will affect what we choose, but we can only blame ourselves if we don't act on our desires, like now for a cigarette, or for a pint – or a girl. Or the excitement of something unexpected, a touch of danger.'

What could he mean? We both sat looking into our empty coffee cups.

'I'd better go,' he said, moving his chair back suddenly and standing, 'or I'll miss the bus.'

'About coming over to see you: how about a Friday?'
'Yes, Friday's fine. We'll fix a date.'

His house was near the middle of a short terrace that ran along the flank of the mountain and marked the limit of human habitation in that place. Other terraces ran up the valley side to this stone and brick and slate-topped buffer at the end of the line. Once you had climbed there, up the steep hill – it wasn't on a bus route – you could look down over the roofs of the parallel rows of dwellings that seemed suspended from it to the black centre of the valley, from which rose in curiously fluctuating volume as the breeze cut across them clangs of metal on metal, the rattle of coal descending chutes and the slow pounding of steam engines.

We walked down the hill again to the Band Club in the evening. The club was popular with miners and the bar comfortably full. Upstairs was the rehearsal room where the colliery silver band practised, but there was no practice that evening. As we pushed open the door my companion was greeted with familiar shouts – 'Richie boy, who's your friend?' 'Go easy tonight.' He smiled and waved cheerily in response. He bought beers and we leaned against a corner of the bar viewing the room. They were playing cards on some tables, smoke from cigarettes and pipes spiraled into the air towards the amber-stained ceiling, and there was a constant buzz of talk and occasional laughter.

'They like to think they are looking after me,' Richie said, '– the older ones. My father was a member here – a bandsman; played the clarinet. They all came to his funeral. I remember that. A huge crowd, all men. And my mother ... in a black coat. And the priest, old Father John it was at that time. The band played in the cemetery, up on the hill across the other side of the valley. It was cold. It had snowed – not much, but a thin covering over the graves and on the top of the gravestones. And the big, old cars – very black against the snow, and footprints trailing up to the open grave.'

He drank deeply, glanced at the half-empty glass and placed it on the bar behind him. An older man came over, stooped, grizzled, with a large nose, huge ears propping up his cap, and thick gnarled hands.

'A pint?' he said. 'Haven't seen you since you're back. How's uni?'

'Fine, Uncle Jack,' Richie said, his accent modified, and he picked up and drained his glass.

'And you, young man?'

'No, thank you very much,' I said, holding up a nearly full pint. 'I'm visiting because we are thinking of going to Spain with two other friends from coll. – if we can get a car cheap.'

'It's not a place I'd go to.' Uncle Jack knew all about Franco. He pushed his cap back and scratched his head. 'There's a few families round here lost husbands or sons or brothers fighting against the bugger,' he said. 'Are you sure they'll let you in?'

'Yes, Uncle Jack, no trouble.'

'And what are you going to do about money – for the car to start with? And don't forget petrol – it won't go without. Are you thinking of eating while you're over there?'

'I'll get a job,' I said, 'straight away, as soon as I come down from coll. in the summer. I worked in a pre-cast concrete factory last year, making slabs and pillars. With any luck they'll take me on again.'

'And I'll go back to grave-digging,' said Richie.

'I'll leave you to your planning,' said Uncle Jack, 'but you be damn careful. Sure you won't have a pint?'

'No, really – thank you all the same,' I said.

'Well, next time,' said Uncle Jack, as a fresh-filled glass was laid on the bar. 'See you later, Richie.'

The old miner, a little stooped and bow-legged, as though from the habit of carrying a heavy load on his broad back, walked over to join friends playing dominoes, and Richie turned to me.

'He's Dad's older brother,' he said. 'They seem to be proud of me. I expect it's because not many round here go to university. Before I went up for my first term they had a collection and raised twelve pounds for me – to buy books, they said, but I'm afraid a fair bit of it went on ...' He lifted the glass and shook his head, as though deprecating his own weakness, and drank.

I could see that, from the day he was first allowed in, he had been a regular there, and still was during vacations. And he was well liked. That was no surprise. It was easy to like Richie. I had never found anyone so easy to talk with. It helped that we were both interested in the literature on the syllabus, which wasn't always the case among others in the class, and we also read books far too modern to be included in an English course in those days: he was for Yeats and Joyce, I read all the American novels I could lay my hands on. And we both

18

thought we would like to become writers. I fiddled with local, familiar things and what I hoped were striking images, while he was for the big themes, love and hate, suicide and murder, life and death. In the end neither of us made it, though he might have done.

Anyway, there was more to it than that. He was the sort of man you knew you could talk to, without feeling any pressure to perform, to put on a face and a manner. Just talk. The sort of man you were immediately at home with, an instant friend. When, after Spain, I eventually returned to college, I found I could no longer stomach English studies, and in an unusual act of generosity for the time, the philosophy department agreed to take me in. There I read the most human of thinkers, Montaigne, and came across lines that have stayed with me. Referring to his all-too-brief friendship as a young man with Étienne de La Boëtie, author of an essay denouncing all forms of dictatorship, full of scholarship and wit, written when he was only eighteen, and dead of dysentery at thirty-two, he says, 'On our first chance meeting at a party in town, we were instantly so familiar, so obliged to one another, that from the selfsame moment we two could not have been closer. If I were pressed to say why I loved him, I could only shrug – "Because it was him; because it was me". Truly, if I compare all the rest of my life to the few years I was given to enjoy the company and society of such a friend, it is nothing but dark, wearying night.'

I remember the first night Richie and I met properly, though I had seen him about coll. – almost always in the centre of a group, and that unmistakeable mellifluous baritone of his carrying. It was early in the second year, in the basement bar of a hotel, a rather smart place where the beer was so expensive you usually didn't linger for more than a pint or two, but the grants had arrived that day. We'd had a lecture on Coleridge, a good opening topic and I had a notion that 'Kubla Khan' was not an opium dream interrupted by a person from Porlock, but a poem, a wonderful poem, created from descriptions of landscape in travel books. I had done geography in the sixth form and knew enough about geomorphology to recognise streams meandering on bands of clay, sink-holes, ravines, underground rivers, lakes cupped between high peaks that rarely see the sun: 'Limestone and clay vales,' I said, with a note of triumph. 'And I can tell you where you can find scenery just like that – in the far north-west of India.' I had once spent hours turning the pages of an atlas looking for a likely spot with just those features.

Richie was impressed. He'd had a couple by then and began reciting the poem quietly while I restrained myself from interrupting with 'There you are, just as I said ...'

'... And drunk the milk of paradise.' – When his voice faded at the end, I realised the bar had gone quiet. Though he spoke low, to me, his voice had carried, everyone had been listening to him. There was no applause (I would have joined in if anyone had started), but the voice and the words had a kind of charm, and he knew it all and recited it quietly and beautifully, with a note of meditative wonder. What followed was silence, but gradually people resumed their small talk and the former atmosphere of the place returned.

At stop tap, warm early autumn with a big moon low

over the rooftops, it seemed a good idea to commune with Nature by walking together barefoot, an experience not entirely spoiled for me by concern about messages left by dogs, which Richie seemed happily oblivious of.

We both had other friends and other things to do in our spare time. I played games, any games – basketball, badminton, snooker, table-tennis. Richie's eyesight was not good, and this may have restricted his sporting options. We played an occasional game of snooker and I used to watch him, glasses on, screwing his eyes up, and squinting along the cue. Even then, often enough he missed his aim. But he was a fine actor, appeared with some distinction in college drama productions and would rush off from the café to rehearsals. From time to time, too, he disappeared at weekends, to go home I supposed at the time, but I was wrong. Regardless of our differences of taste and temperament, our conversation continued from that first evening. Whenever we were together outside the lecture room, over coffee, having a beer, walking around or out of town, skipping smooth stones across the river, we picked up the thread, and carried on as though there had been no pause.

We left the Band Club just after ten o'clock that evening. I remember my first steps were like walking on cushions, but the night air and the effort of tackling the hill did wonders for the concentration. Richie, who was perfectly steady, though he had drunk a good deal more, was reciting Dylan Thomas poems to the darkened street and the night sky, and we walked to the cadence of the verses. He had the voice to do Dylan Thomas, and I loved listening to him, but it was late.

'Not so loud,' I said, 'not so loud. People trying to sleep. I didn't know you'd been digging graves.'

'Yes, last summer – to give the regular lads holiday time. You should try it – good for the muscles.' He flexed his biceps strong-man style, and laughed.

'"Alas, poor Yorick ..." and so on.'

'No sign of skulls, or bones of any kind. It was virgin cemetery soil, right up near the top of the ridge. Very pleasant in fine weather. I was working with one of the older lads, in his fifties I should think, and he used to go down the pub for a pint or two at lunchtime, while I stayed with sandwiches and a flask of tea. A pint appealed to me too, but I didn't want to drink my wages before I had them. We had just about finished digging one morning, down about five feet, and no one was about, so I dropped into the hole and just lay down there, looking up. You know that engraving of Donne, still alive, in his shroud?'

I shook my head, but he carried on.

'Well, I thought I'd do the same sort of thing. So I lay there a while, on my back, arms behind my head, looking up, through this slot, at the sky, a summer sky, blue, with clouds lazing by. Red earth, a bit mucky, but quite restful. So this is what it's like, I thought – from here you go through that gap there, beyond those tumbling clouds, all the way to heaven. Daft.'

The house in the top terrace was in darkness. Richie's mother had gone to bed. There were some corned-beef sandwiches on the kitchen table and a bottle of milk standing in cold water in the sink. I didn't think I was hungry, but with the first bite hunger arrived.

An iron-framed single bed had been made up for me in a small back bedroom, the curtains already drawn. Over the bedhead hung a simple wooden cross and over the washstand in the corner an image of Christ pulling aside the blue cloak covering his shoulders to reveal a glowing heart pulsing bright shafts of light. That was the first time I had seen the Sacred Heart and it brought home the reach and hold of Catholicism. The bed jangled as I entered between the sheets. I lay still and, waiting for sleep, turned over what Richie's uncle had said about Franco. The name was familiar and I'd heard about the Spanish Civil War, but knew nothing of Welsh involvement in it. Perhaps the old man had exaggerated, though he didn't look the sort. No one in school had mentioned the war in Spain, not even who was fighting whom. Only that Franco's side won. It was as though World War Two had erased everything before it. But then, I didn't know either what had gone on in south Wales in the 1920s and 1930s, except that there was a strike in 1926. My parents, who had lived through those years, never spoke of the decades of strife and hardship, and school history lessons were about the Ancient Egyptians and the Normans, never a word about Wales, a conundrum I was too tired to contemplate.

I slept better than I anticipated and woke to daylight suffusing the room. It was just after seven o'clock and there were sounds of activity elsewhere in the house. I opened the curtains and was startled to find the mountain rising steeply like a blotched green wall at what seemed touching distance beyond the pane. Richie's valley was narrower, steeper-sided than mine, and the house seemed built into it. An urgent need to relieve my bladder cut short further observation of the scene. The lavatory was out the back and I put trousers and jacket on over my pyjamas for the excursion. I crept back up the stairs to the bedroom, where there was a bowl and a pitcher of water on the washstand with a new half-bar of green soap and a small towel. It was what I was used to away from home, for there was no bathroom in my digs at college. I washed and dressed myself properly and sat on the bed looking out at the mountain, where sheep were grazing. In a while, Richie's mother called from the foot of the stairs. I heard a muffled response, counted a hundred, and went down slowly.

In morning light, I saw the faded picture of highland cattle hanging in the hall, the brown, patterned oilcloth on the floor, everything worn, but clean. Anything capable of shining shone. The kitchen was the same: the fireplace gleaming with black lead and polished brass, a rag rug on the hearth. Richie's mother was pulling a rope to raise the clothes-dryer rack close to the ceiling and, as she did so revealing another picture that I hadn't noticed the previous evening. This was a dark scene of a man in a battered tall hat and ragged top coat, a long gun over his shoulder, a dead rabbit hanging from one hand – a poacher, I guessed – looking at an unkempt, weeping woman holding a limp baby, and underneath, words I have been unable to forget, 'The Fruits of Idleness'. What a terrible warning, I thought, more Puritan than Catholic.

Richie's mother was tall and slight. Her thin-lipped, angular features had been passed on to her son, like the dark hair, but hers had faded iron-grey and was pulled back tight from her face. She seemed worn and weary but determined to be welcoming. I don't know what money came into the home – not much anyway: a widow's pension. Richie, an only child, had a good student grant but brought nothing in, unless from his holiday work. I didn't think of this at the time, or the possibility, likelihood even, that his mother took in washing, or went out cleaning for other people, to make a bit extra. She made sure I had a good breakfast before I left – bacon and egg, and chips. A lot of chips. I had never had chips for breakfast before and thought I'd gone to heaven. She'd risen early, made up the fire and done all the peeling and chipping before we stirred.

Richie walked me down to the bus stop and we had our discussion about the trip to Spain on the way. Alan was committed to another continental trip, alone or with others, whatever the destination –Spain preferred, and once he was satisfied Evelyn would neither stand in the way of it nor go out with someone else in his absence, Gwyn was in favour. For him, the expense involved was not a problem.

'Mam will miss the couple of bob my summer job brings in,' Richie said, 'but I know if I ask her she'll say, "Go on – we'll manage without that. We've done it before".'

I had already asked my mother, who made all the decisions in our house, and she had said it was up to me, so long as I paid my own way. 'Only take care. Take care.'

'How about it then? I'd really rather like to see Spain,' I said, with an unexpected surge of enthusiasm. 'Let's go, is it?'

Richie looked surprised, and then he laughed. 'All right then, if you're up for it, so long as the cost of the car won't make too big a hole in the term's grant. The rest should take care of itself. Or Alan will look after it.'

That was the first independent commitment of my life, and the one I have most regretted. We shook hands as the bus came in. On the way home I thought of Richie lying in the open grave, the pile of shovelled earth waiting.

I should have remembered at once, as soon as the photographs tumbled out of the box, that they were all taken on the journey south. The Madrid signpost snap was the last. I didn't buy another roll of film. The most evocative of the best of times that summer, certainly the clearest, is one that was taken by Gwyn, who may have had some experience of photography, or luck in the way he focused on the subject and allowed the background to take care of itself – which it did handsomely. This time it's of Alan, Richie and me leaning against the car, neatly just off-centre in the foreground. For once you can see our faces clearly, and the number plate of the car: MG2013. Behind, the long, straight, empty road is edged on both sides with a row of tall poplars. It summons up France, the south, the sun, in those post-war years when Europe was still clearing up wartime devastation. Outside the larger towns, apart from tinny Citroen 2CVs pressed into a variety of uses, motor vehicles of any sort passed infrequently, and people viewed a foreign car with surprise and wonder.

Apart from its evident oddity there, our car was

unremarkable. It was already a veteran, though not of continental travel, first registered in 1932, in the days when cars were meant to last and, given reasonable care, usually did. It cost us sixty pounds, fifteen pounds each. My fifteen came from the little that was left of my college grant for the Easter term and savings from holiday work delivering mail. My father thought even a share in a car was a big step and was keen to know where exactly it had come from. Was it reliable? he asked, and did any of us know anything about the internal combustion engine before we trusted the car and ourselves to a long journey? 'Do any of you have a driving licence?'

To the last question and all those preceding there was only one answer – Alan. He had a licence, had acquired basic skills in car mechanics as a soldier, and he knew about travel in Europe having wandered widely there since demob. He had also found the car. It belonged to a farmer, who had bought it new and now, rather sadly, was prepared to let it go. He lived a couple of miles out of town.

On a lustrous spring day, one weekend in the summer term, before the business of exam preparation became urgent, we walked out to view the car. The sky was cloudless and hedges, already in full leaf, were shimmering in variegated greens and busy with birds. Where the hedge was interrupted by a broad field gate we stood and looked across a meadow yellow with buttercups to the other side of the valley and blue hills beyond. A small distance off, where the field began to slope away, was a clump of well-grown trees so close-planted that with their sturdy trunks coalesced and massed foliage they appeared a well-risen loaf of green bread. We were all very cheerful. As the others turned aside and moved on, meditatively, almost to himself, Richie said, 'If ever there were promise of a good outcome to a project, it is surely here in the warmth of the sun and a sense of levitation, things on the rise, as the breeze stirs branches and shining leaves.'

'A poetic observation,' I muttered, though I don't think he heard me. 'I hope you're right.'

We were the best of friends, if you accept friendship is not without its share of envy and rivalry. We constantly talked together, mostly about the course and the other books outside the course we were reading. Whenever I could, I took a different line from him, and we argued in class, where we were usually the quickest to raise questions, and offer answers.

I was never short of friends at home; my fondness of games and a normal ability to kick or hit a ball more or less accurately took care of that. But none of the friendships was close, perhaps because I was almost always among the youngest in the group. My mother and father were surprised when I, their second child, was born, for my sister was twelve. 'You were an afterthought,' my mother used to say, which was kinder than 'accident'. I was told my sister resented my arrival and the demands that a new baby in the family made of her, but she grew out of that. Eventually we became very close, so that I knew I could depend on her, as she could have done on me, though she never asked. But, of course, she was a girl and soon a young woman, sensible and caring, then married and away. Almost as soon as I had any sense of self I was to all intents and purposes an only child. I was loved, and spoilt perhaps.

I was not lonely, because there were other boys living opposite our house and in neighbouring rows. Among the pairs of brothers I roamed the mountain and played games with, there were some who bullied younger siblings to the point of protest, anger and tears, but more often I observed the older showing the younger how to hold a bat or grip a ball, or sharing with him boyhood lore and intimacies from which I was excluded. I think I envied them their deep knowledge of one another, the readiness of the more experienced in life to encourage and, whenever necessary, protect the one who followed behind. I was among the youngest in our year at college, too. Hero-worship and the desire to emulate came perhaps too readily to me. I know that's no excuse: time is a marginal factor only in growth to maturity. But, looking back, I prefer to think it was youth that caused me to be drawn to Richie. At least, that is how I try to explain to myself and excuse the black prostration of the spirit that overwhelmed me at the end of that summer so long ago.

The first sign of the farm was a sturdy wooden platform built into the bank at the top of a narrow dirt lane that, within fifty yards, fell abruptly away. Grass grew tall between the ruts worn by the regular passage of farm vehicles. The platform was designed to hold two or three milk churns ready for collection. When we passed it was empty: the full churns had been collected by the milk lorry, the empty ones left in their place already retrieved by the farmer ready for the next day's milking. As we walked down the dip we seemed to enter a dark passage. The bank on either side grew taller and the hedges at the top of the bank leaned inwards. Spring showers had been unusually sparse that year and it was dry underfoot when in the wet it would have been slippery, but we were glad when we reached the bottom of the hill. There the view opened out and in a slight hollow before us was the whitewashed farmhouse and its outbuildings clustered around a modest-sized yard, where some chickens were scratching and picking at the dust.

We had barely touched the yard gate when a black and white sheepdog rose from the dark doorway of a barn and bounded, barking, towards us. In a moment or two, Davies, the farmer, ruddy cheeked, a cap askew on his head, emerged from a gate at the top of some steps. He was in his shirt sleeves, braces holding up stained breeches, muscular forearms, open collar, a V of white hairy chest. Behind a wall, we could see the upper floor of the farm and its slate roof. A trail of grey smoke rose from the chimney. With a sign and a word, he brought the dog to heel.

'Don't you worry, she's a good dog – aren't you, Meg?' He bent to pat her head and the bitch looked up, one eye brown, the other blue, tongue lolling, and wagged her tail.

'And you've come about the car.' He had a crooked gap-toothed smile. 'She's in the barn.'

He led the way to another dark doorway and opened

wide the second door to light the interior. 'Come and look her over. I'll be sorry to see her go, but go she must, I don't want her rusting away here – not that there's any fault with her, bit dirty, that's all – still a low mileage after twenty-two years. You look.'

He motioned us to the car, which had been black but was grey with dust and decorated with wisps of straw and bird droppings from nests in the rafters. Chickens strayed in and out between the wheels.

'I don't need her now. Used to take my old Mam to the market in her, but she died a few months back – and I just got a small tractor, who'll do the job as well, better probably in the winter, and be useful for other things about the farm.'

That the connection was not immediately apparent he must have read in our faces. 'She's worked for me over the years and never given a moment's trouble,' he went on. 'This is only a small farm – a one-man farm – but I've got a few cows, you know, and the dairy lorry comes in the morning to pick up the churns at the top of the lane. Well, I lash the churns on that sort of grid thing you can lower down at the back,' he pointed to the frame folded up against the spare wheel, ' – it's meant for carrying – and off she goes up the lane. Can take that hill like a bird. In first. Always starts, as long as you treat her properly. Do you want to try her? She's got a six-volt battery, but she hasn't had a run for a few weeks, so we'd better use the starting handle. Come on, I'll give her a crank for you.'

Alan brushed off straw clinging to the windscreen and sat behind the wheel.

'Give her a bit of choke, not too much, when she begins to fire, then full out when she catches – and quickly in again. You know what I mean?'

'Yes, OK.'

The farmer stooped and, spreading his gaitered legs, grasped the starting handle. He swung it up quite easily a couple of times, then, 'Now she's catching,' he said, and with a grunt swung again, sharply.

The engine spluttered, then roared in the confines of the barn. A small cloud of grey smoke rose from the exhaust, chickens flew squawking out into the yard and the sheepdog barked, wagging its tail.

'There you are – told you she'd start.' The farmer looked relieved. 'Right Meg, that's enough,' he said. 'She likes to ride up the lane with me. Sits up in the front seat, looking out of the windscreen, just like a lady.'

After coaxing the engine to a steady rattling beat, Alan switched off the ignition and emerged smiling. 'I think we'll manage her,' he said.

'Yes, it's quite warm for the time of year, thank goodness,' said the farmer. 'You have to be a bit patient with her in the winter, mind. I put old blankets over the bonnet to keep her warm. If you've got a garage, I'd get one of those little paraffin burners and put it underneath the engine when it's frosty.'

Alan looked doubtful. 'Might be dangerous with petrol about. Anyway, where we're going it will be warm enough. We'll probably be able to rely on the battery.' He turned to us, 'What do you think, will this car do?'

I knew nothing about cars, but it looked roomy enough for the four of us. If Alan, who seemed familiar with the intricacies of their workings, was satisfied, I had no complaint.

'It will be fine,' said Richie, in buoyant mood. 'Yes, absolutely fine.'

Smiling, Gwyn added his agreement and, with the slightest qualm about travelling further from home than ever before, I nodded my content with the role of passenger.

'It's time to pay up then,' said Alan. 'Sixty pounds the ad said?'

There would be no haggling: the farmer looked pleased and the dog came and rubbed herself against his legs as we each counted out our fifteen pound shares into his broad palm.

'Where's she going to take you?'

We told him we would be going in August to France and then Spain. 'Well, well. France and Spain,' he said, looking bewildered. He lifted his cap to scratch his thinning, crinkled thatch and patted the dusty bonnet affectionately, 'France and Spain – a big change for you from going up and down that old lane.' He shook our hands in turn. 'Good luck then, boys,' he said.

The car started at once and Alan drove us out of the yard, the dog chasing us as far as the gate, barking furiously, up the steep lane in first and back to town. The gearbox was giving him some trouble he said, but it was the sort of thing you might expect. You needed to get used to a car's foibles, coax it a bit. He dropped us off at the students' union and carried on home. He had been born and bred in the town and lived with his widowed mother in a cottage with a garden that backed onto the river, not far from one of the main bridges. There was no garage; he parked it outside, and that's where we found him and the car some days later.

He had cleaned the vehicle inside and out and it appeared in remarkably good shape for its age, the black bodywork free of bumps and scratches, plenty of tread on the tyres, and the rexine-covered seats, apart from the driver's, almost pristine. It had done its share of heavy work carrying milk churns up a steep hill, but otherwise, as the farmer said, had been little used. The milometer supported that view: in over twenty years, the car had covered only fifteen thousand miles. The war, when petrol for private use was restricted or unavailable, and after the war, until 1954, while it remained rationed, partly explained that.

It appeared we'd had a bargain, though, as Alan had immediately recognised, there was a problem with the gears. This was probably the reason the farmer had decided to sell. Chiefly for Gwyn's benefit, because he was being taught to drive by his father and had a provisional licence, he explained, 'Second gear's shot – most of that driving loaded uphill was probably in second. But give her a good run in first and you can go straight into third. Just three forward gears. OK?' Gwyn looked rather dubious, but nodded.

'There you are,' said Richie, 'no problem at all really.'

Gwyn was less sanguine. 'That's all very well, but you won't be driving.'

Oh, I'll have a try, while we're in France – or Spain, you'll see.' Smiling, he slapped Gwyn on the back. 'You'll see.'

Our black 1932 Morris didn't stand out. Most of the cars on the road were old, and black. Most of them also appeared box-like. Our motorised box had two doors each side opening from a central pillar, and running boards angled from the narrow back mudguards to broad sweeping wings at the front, the model's only curves. Sidelights were perched on the wings and a pair of goggle-eyed headlights were mounted either side of the bonnet. The radiator-cap incorporated a temperature gauge, glazed, about the size of a matchbox. A driver with good eyesight could just about make out the angle of the needle from inside the car to check if the engine was over-heating. That it was an attractive feature we eventually found out in Spain.

Richie and I were the first in our families to own, or part-own, a car. When he was younger, my father had a motorbike, but I had no memory of it. From time to time, he would say 'I wish we had a car then we could all go off for a trip, a picnic or something, if it was a nice day.' And my mother would say, 'Well, it looks as though it's going to rain anyway.' But he liked the idea of a car, a car with a big engine, because a big engine would last longer, he said. But it was all fantasy; we couldn't afford a car of any sort. Only one other student, apart from us, had a car. It was said his father owned a garage (or was it a cinema?), anyway, had a lot of money. He brought it up one summer term and it stood neglected outside his digs. You really didn't need a car in college, so what was the point?

Of the journey through England to Newhaven on the south coast I remember nothing, and little remains of my impressions on stepping ashore for the first time in France. Distantly, in my mind's eye, Dieppe is a vague jumble of harbour and grey town on a grey day, and perhaps a huge concrete gun emplacement, abandoned by the retreating Wehrmacht and still frowning above the sea nine years after the war. Or have I invented that? Memory is a fallible faculty at best, and all this occurred a long time ago. Fragments separate, merge and coalesce. One image calls up another from a different time and it's not always easy to explain the connection. And then all the randomness is one stream without order or logic. I curse myself that I kept only the scrappiest record of part of our route, nothing of what we saw and did. It had been my ambition then to be a writer, so why didn't I write when everything was fresh, painfully fresh? Because when we got home, all I wanted to do was forget it.

On the road through France we made better progress than Alan expected. The rest of us had no expectations. While Richie and I contributed nothing to the journey but an occasional commentary on the passing scene, Gwyn had his provisional licence and the benefit of a few lessons. Whether this would have been enough to satisfy the gendarmerie that he was competent behind the wheel, Alan was unsure, but he could change gear and steer, and was allowed to take over where the roads were straight and clear, which, outside towns and villages, they usually were.

Once Dieppe was behind us, the weather was sunny and hot and we were glad the Morris had a primitive form of air-conditioning. The front windscreen could be opened at the base and tilted outwards so that while we were moving there was a constant flow of air through the car. Even so, as we got farther south, Alan often drove stripped to the waist, every rib so distinct you could have played the xylophone on them.

The route between Dieppe and Paris is a blank, the memory bank broken open and all content pilfered by time, but of Paris there are memories. We must have parked the car somewhere in the centre of the city, close to the Seine – parking restrictions hardly existed then. Perhaps it was near Notre Dame or Place de la Concorde, within easy distance of the Champs Élysées, for that is where we walked, on the great, broad thoroughfare leading up to the Arc de Triomphe. I recall the sense of spaciousness and tall buildings, windows gilded by evening light. We were strolling up the long hill together, taking out time, four abreast, for there was plenty of room on what seemed to be an inner, traffic-free road. And then the sun was sinking behind the tall buildings. It was becoming dusk; some shop windows were lit and streetlights coming on. There were very few vehicles of any kind, and what there were moved without haste on a broader highway to our left. It was warm, a foretaste of the summer heat we would experience later. The City of Light seemed half-awake or was it half-asleep. We were nearing the top, the great open area of the Étoile, where several roads converge, when we became aware that a rather splendid black limousine was following close behind us. How long it had moved quietly, at walking pace, pausing when we paused, it is impossible to know, for the driver did not sound the horn, roll the window down and shout, or give the least sign. With apologetic gestures we stepped aside to allow the car to pass, which it did quietly, slowly. A maelstrom of traffic now roars constantly about the Étoile and forms two unbroken lines along the Champs Élysées, but not then, not in 1954.

We were close to the top of the hill, the great arch more imposingly large with each step, when we came upon a group of young women gathered at a street corner, They were lightly dressed, in garments that might have been of silk or chiffon, in summery colours, yellow, pink, light blue. Their hair, dark or fair, hung loose about their shoulders, and they smiled and arched their eyebrows as though they recognised and were about to greet us.

Richie was instantly bowled over. He took off and rubbed his glasses with his handkerchief, then replaced them and smiled. 'What lovely-looking girls. Let's stop and talk.'

He turned to the young women and performed an elaborate theatrical bow. One of them lifted her gauzy skirt to her thighs and curtsied in return, and they all laughed and made beckoning gestures. 'Look, they fancy our company. Alan, you can speak to them. Tell them we're new here, strangers, never been in Paris before. Ask if they can recommend somewhere to have a drink. I could do with a drink.'

Gwyn had turned away and was looking in a shop window, but I was equally fascinated. They were like no young women I had ever seen before – except in films – and seemed gracefully at ease, speaking among themselves, looking frankly at us with amused expressions, then laughing together.

'Alan, Alan, say something to them before they go off somewhere else. Come on, they won't bite.'

But Alan wasn't smiling. 'I don't think you want to get to know them.'

'Well, I do. I'll speak to them myself.'

'I wouldn't advise it. Really. They'll want money and, tempting as the prospect may be, I'm fairly certain you can't afford to go to a bar with them. They're nymphs of the pave, street walkers – prostitutes.'

Richie looked dumbfounded, and crestfallen. 'But they're lovely.'

'H'm, yes, you're right, very smart, attractive at this distance, though perhaps less wholesome as you get closer. You wouldn't be the first on a tour abroad to fall for one. But it's a trap. I've had to pick up the pieces a few times when we were serving in Germany in the years after the war.'

Gwyn caught Richie by the sleeve and pulled him away. 'This will only lead to trouble.'

Richie shook him off. 'Oh, come on,' he said. 'Talk to them, anyway. Let's just have a bit of fun.'

'I think we'd better go and find a quiet place off this road, where we can get a drink that won't cost half the price you'd have to pay here.'

'I'd rather a noisy place, with some real life in it. What's the point of coming to Paris?'

I remember I felt much the same as Richie. The rest of that evening and our overnight in Paris have been erased, but the vision of the young women, gaudy under

the streetlamp at that street corner on the Champs
Élysées, left a lingering impression on me, like an
unfulfilled promise, and stayed to trouble Richie.

'It's no more than I expected of Gwyn. But I like
Alan,' he confided to me later. 'This is the trip of a
lifetime. Not many people where we come from go
abroad, unless they're in the army – and that's not
much fun. Think of the First World War, and the poor
buggers Uncle Jack knew later who went to Spain to
fight against Franco. And there's Alan – a soldier!' He
shook his head. 'Yes, I like him a lot. Only he's not my
Dad. And he's a man of the world... seen it all. I
thought he'd be ready for a bit of fun. Just talking to
them. If he was right and they were pros, I couldn't
have afforded the pleasure anyway. Ah, lovely thought:
that would be something to confess to Father Trevor. I
hope Alan won't keep warning me off. Off whatever. I
want to find out for myself. If it all goes wrong, I'll
know who to blame.'

I thought about Richie's irritation afterwards, as I lay
waiting for sleep to come. Alan was a good ten years
older than us and, though he wore it lightly, this
seniority was of no commonplace kind. He had seen
action, witnessed horrors that we, for all the newsreels of
battles and liberated concentration camps, had hardly the
slightest conception of. It was difficult to imagine his
slight figure in khaki, with a gun. The bony face,
prominent eyes, wide, thin-lipped mouth were far better
suited to monkish garb – hair shirt, scapular and cowl. I
am sure he had no wish to be a father-figure to us; an
older brother, perhaps, whom I would have been glad to

have. With the single exception of that Paris evening, all of us were content to accept the authority he wore lightly.

Early the following morning, before we left Paris, Alan said we would follow the N20 all the way to the Pyrénées and Spain. It made sense to aim for Orleans as our first stop, about sixty miles. The chief town on our route after that was Limoges, another 150 miles beyond, out of our reach that day.

We studied the map together. The obvious place to head for, after seeing a bit of the town and lunch at Orleans, if we made reasonable time, was Vierzon.

'How about Bourges?'

We looked at Alan. 'It's a bit farther,' said Gwyn, 'and off the N20. It will make a longer day.'

He was right, Bourges was at least twenty miles southeast of Vierzon.

'Something I want you to see there – the cathedral, perched at the very top of the old town, which climbs up a hill towards it. The bottom of the hill, where a new town has grown, is quite flat and marshy in parts. Buildings there were battered a bit in the war. It got caught because there's an airfield a couple of miles out and all the fighting was over that. It was a particular target of the German advance in 1940 and took a hammering from allied planes and artillery in '44. Our lot didn't get down that way, but I've visited since, just to see the cathedral. It has wonderful stained glass, medieval, still intact. You ought to see it.'

We were easily persuaded. 'You're the driver,' Richie

said, '– if you don't mind going the extra miles, it's OK by me.'

We settled ourselves in the Morris and the road with the sun upon it stretched straight before us like a silver line, narrowing in the distance to a point. Late afternoon it must have been (how long the journey I no longer remember), a roadside sign announced Bourges.

Alan was right. The cathedral crowned a hill and climbing the narrow, winding streets we caught only occasional glimpses of it, so that when we emerged on the open square at the top, the immensity of the stone cliff intricately decorated with images, and the tower soaring skywards like a rocket aimed at heaven, were almost shocking. The massive wooden door closed with an echoing crash and as silence flowed slowly back, Alan led us to the tower stairs, hundreds of stone steps spiraling upwards, each one dented in the middle as by a giant thumb. From the top the close-knitted, tiled roofs of the old town were a patchwork of faded red corduroy, and beyond 'the vasty fields of France' stretched away into the distance. It was my first experience of religious awe. What power of God – and man – to have created so vast a structure, what daring to think it into being, what skill to shape and fit block to block, what weight of stone and wood to lift and put in place!

Returned to the nave, the pale masonry surrounding us gleamed, beautiful and good. We were all subdued. It was not a place for talk. Strong early evening sun slanting through ancient stained-glass projected pools of coloured light on a floor polished by centuries of humbly shuffling feet. Occasional distant, quiet voices told us others were present somewhere in the enormous soaring space, but there was no one to be seen as we walked towards the gilded altar. Richie, too, or perhaps most of all, was affected by the place. He had dropped behind and I turned to see him genuflect and cross himself, and then, his eye caught by something, peer to his left.

'Come and see this,' he said.

He pointed to a patch of floor where, as we looked more closely, what at first appeared random marks on the white marble organised themselves into carefully incised connecting patterns of circles and squares, and ruled lines.

'They look like plans. Could they be of this building?'

Gwyn rubbed his chin thoughtfully, while I tried to gather my wits.

'Yes, it's certainly something to do with this building,' Alan said. 'What part exactly I've no notion, but some anonymous medieval master-mason knelt here to scratch a plan of next week's work for builders and carpenters and the rest of his crew.'

'They must have been making it up as they went along,' I said.

'When you think of what they needed to know – of geometry and ratio and proportion – with just plumb bobs and string and rulers, it is staggering. Not to mention raising huge blocks of stone a hundred feet or more,' he paused and gazed upwards, ' – and putting them... *exactly* into place.'

'How on earth did they manage it without cranes and machinery?' Gwyn was nonplussed.

Richie laughed. 'Ah, but they had the power of prayer, and God as the foreman of works.'

The windows glowed in the caught light, exquisitely beautiful, but it took a little time to grasp their cartoon narratives. Some were, to us, indecipherable, but we recognised the obvious: there was Christ's entry into Jerusalem, there the Last Supper, there the Crucifixion. Another told about the Prodigal Son, and another the Good Samaritan. Here lay a dying man, and in the corner opposite the dead rising from their tombs. Above these images, the good were ascending to Paradise, and on the other side the tortured souls of sinners were being swallowed in the mouth of Hell.

'I can just see the old priest ramming home the messages to the crowd around him. "You carry on as you are and that's what will happen".' Richie's voice echoed around the vast space. 'Poor sods.'

We came upon the stairway to the crypt as we were making our way out. After the exaltation of vaulted roof, arches, glorious windows, symbolic wood carving, sculpted saints and prophets in niches it came as a surprise. All the religious high art was brought crashing down by a display of earthiness in the marble busts above the handrail either side of the stair.

Gwyn, peering at one of the portraits said, 'I don't think I have ever seen so blatant an expression of desire. What does he want – a place in the Church, wealth, position?'

'No, it's sex.' Richie pointed to the sweet-faced, bosomy woman on the other side of the stair. 'He's lusting after her. Look, his eyes are fixed on her.'

'She isn't looking at him,' I said. 'She's gazing at the handsome young fellow next to the old lecher.'

'You're right. And whose fine buttocks are these?' Richie laughed. 'Definitely male. I know what this reminds me of. It's Nicholas's arse ... in "The Miller's Tale". We've got a double frieze of Canterbury pilgrims in marble. Do you think Chaucer found his inspiration in France?'

'The Miller's Tale' had never turned up in a syllabus, but Richie and I had read it when Coghill's translation of *The Canterbury Tales* came out. He had just bought a copy and we sat on a bench on the riverbank, knowing what to look for, and read it together, hooting with laughter.

'Why don't we get to work on texts like this? That would liven up class discussion.'

'I'm not sure it would,' I said. 'Most of us are squeamish; don't like talking about sex, and arses and farting. The girls wouldn't say a word. And who would teach it? But as I spoke I was thinking of O'Brien, a new lecturer on the Shakespeare course, who had pointed at me and said, laughing, 'You're too young to read *Measure for Measure*', which guaranteed that I read it at once. On another occasion I remember how he had dismissed as useless reviews of Shakespeare productions in the Sunday broadsheets, which we treated with reverence. 'If you want to get a hold on Shakespeare, read the *News of the World* – "All human life is there".'

We were still laughing as we headed downhill to the parked car. Nearby was a cheap auberge where we found two rooms for the night. A bar a few steps across the road offered a simple menu and there seemed little point in looking further. The wine was not to our taste. I had a Romantic notion of wine, for which Keats was largely to blame – 'a beaker full of the warm south' and so on – that the reality was never likely to match, but Richie and the others also found it harsh. It was there, I recall, Alan introduced us to Cinzano Bianco topped up with Perrier by way of substitute.

Later, in a bed that sagged deeply in the middle, so that in sleep I seemed to be rolling downhill, or struggling up, I thought how the medieval sculptors, left to their own devices, had abandoned the pious imagery the Church commanded in praise of God and for the instruction of His people and offered up simple, base humanity – lustful men and coquettish women, clowns and hypocrites, the shy and the brazen, gloating evil and indifference. Alone with my conscience, I was unsure whether to laugh again, or to weep for our frailties. I said my prayers, as always, not aloud, not even in a whisper, but silently, in my mind. I was sure that God, if there was a God, could hear or see the words, as they passed there, soft prints on snow at the edge of sleep. I had habitually from childhood addressed my pleas to Him for the things I desired, my parents' and my sister's health, success at football or exams, the girl I had fallen romantically in love with – mostly childish things that had lingered on into young manhood, as though God was Father Christmas. This prayerful slipping away to sleep was nothing to do with faith or belief, just child-like wishful thinking, but harmless, secret. And I wondered what Richie, sleeping peacefully the other side of the room, made of it all.

The next morning, after more than an hour on the road, we reached Chateauroux and the N20, which would take us to Limoges. I remember the day well. It was cloudless and hot, with hardly a breath, and promised to get hotter. We were bowling along, Richie and I in the back and Gwyn driving with Alan alongside him in case anything unexpected occurred. Gwyn's driving, Alan said, was perfectly fine. He was in command of the dodgy second gear and there was little traffic to be wary of. The road was straight for mile after mile between ranks of tall trees, then there would be a bend or two, often at or near a village, before it recovered its undeviating trajectory south.

Gwyn, sufficiently at ease behind the wheel to take note of the few simple dials on the dashboard, called Alan's attention to the petrol gauge. 'We're running low,' he said. 'Better stop at the next petrol station.'

Alan was calm. 'There's a can in the boot and I'd like to find out how many miles we are doing to the gallon, to get some idea of overall cost, how far we can *afford* to go. So carry on until the tank runs out, then I'll put in the gallon from the can and check the mile counter when the dial shows we need another fill. OK, you in the back?'

'Yes, fine.'

Anything Alan said concerning the car was always OK with Richie and me. We leaned forward to watch the needle on the petrol dial fall to zero, but soon tired of that. A few miles farther on, the engine began to splutter and lose power. Though expected, the silence when it cut out was a shock. Gwyn brought the car coasting to the verge and pulled up the handbrake. We were at one of those bends in the route, but no place-name sign was visible. Behind us, a tree-lined ribbon of asphalt stretched back straight and true into the hazy distance. Nearby, on its surface lay the mirage of a large pool above which the air wavered. Ahead the road climbed a long, gradual ascent, at the top of which it seemed to bend once more out of sight.

Alan retrieved the petrol can from the boot, unscrewed the cap and very carefully poured the entire gallon into the tank. 'Right,' he said, 'ready to go.'

We got into the car as before, Gwyn behind the wheel. He turned the key to start the car. There was the usual whirring of the starter motor, but the engine refused to fire. He tried again. After the fourth attempt, Alan, looking somewhat perplexed, said, 'With the engine still warm, it should have started first time. Perhaps a bit of dirt in the petrol can has blocked the pipe.'

We all got out of the car and watched as he opened the bonnet, detached the petrol feed from the carburettor, blew hard into it, spat on the verge, and blew again. 'Let's give it another try,' he said. 'I'll have a go.'

Behind the wheel, he rubbed his hands briskly, flexed his fingers and turned the key. The starter motor whirred – a little unconvincingly – and the engine refused to start.

'That's it, we're stuck,' said Gwyn. 'It was bound to happen sometime. We're lucky to have got this far. But I wish it could have been in a town. Now what are we going to do? No traffic. No one coming along who might be able to give us a tow. And what if the engine's wrecked?'

Richie laughed at Gwyn's dejected, dismal assessment.

'We'll die out here in the wilds,' he said. 'They'll find four skeletons by a rusted hulk.'

'There's no need for that,' Alan said. 'It's very likely there's a village ahead where we can get help. Probably we'll find a petrol station where we can fill up and that may well disperse any dirt in the tank. I think then the engine will start. In any case, with luck, we'll find a mechanic there. But we've got to get up the hill. There's only one thing for it. Ready to push?'

There seemed little point in discussing further. He resumed his place in the driver's seat and, as best we could, we readied ourselves for the task. The sun beat down, the long upward slope stretched out ahead. We were sweating before Alan released the handbrake. The first combined shove took us forward about fifty yards before we faltered and Alan put on the brake, the next about thirty yards and, after that, breathless, with aching shoulders and thighs, we continued the ascent in gradually diminishing stages. It seemed an age before we reached the sign announcing the hoped-for village ahead. I have no recollection of the name. My head was spinning, my breath rasped in my throat. I believe at that point we three were incapable of any mental process. But Alan had been right: at the top of the hill the village, hamlet rather, lay ahead of us, straddling the road, and, mercifully, a petrol station at the very beginning of the short main street. We pushed the car to a pump on the forecourt and leaned against it panting, beyond speech.

'Well done. Good job! I knew you could do it.' Every bit the soldier, Alan tucked his shirt into his trousers, straightened himself and walked smartly to the overalled proprietor, who was ambling forward from the shade of an awning overhanging the front of his office. We observed them beret to beret, talking together. The Frenchman greeted us with a broad grin and proceeded to fill the tank, while Alan opened the bonnet.

There was a pause as he peered inside at the engine, followed by a suppressed exclamation, and he busied himself for a few moments before turning to us.

'Ah, Gwyn,' he said, 'try her again now, will you?'

Gwyn wiped his sweaty hands, seated himself behind the wheel and turned the key. The starting motor whirred and the engine at once burst into life. 'It worked,' he shouted. 'You were right, Alan.'

'Miracle cure,' said Richie.

We were all mightily relieved. Alan paid for the petrol from the kitty and the Frenchman, still grinning, waved, 'Bon voyage'.

With the windscreen raised, all windows open, the air streamed around us as we sat drying, stiff and salty, in our seats.

In a little while, 'It was worth the pushing,' Gwyn said, and Richie and I in the back agreed wholeheartedly.

'Yes,' Alan said. Then, 'Sorry about that.'

'Well, it had to be done,' Gwyn insisted. 'It *had* to be done.'

'I'm afraid not. You remember I blew down the feed pipe to clear it.'

'And it didn't work. Not your fault.'

'It did actually. Work, I mean. But I'm afraid, what with one thing and another, I forgot to re-connect it to the carburettor.'

Richie was still chuckling intermittently about Alan's uncharacteristic oversight (So he was not immune from failure!) when we drove into Limoges. There were no further attempts to find out how many miles the Morris could do to the gallon. 'It must be about thirty,' Alan said, 'and at that rate we should be covered by the kitty, so long as we don't go in for a lot of diversions. Let's leave it at that.'

My recall of the journey south of Limoges has faded. It was a time of quivering heat, evanescent, dream-like. The names Brive and Cahors linger, but of those towns little beyond the vaguest impression. From the day of the great push, the sun was pitiless. We felt the baking intensity must end soon in an almighty storm, but next morning the bright orb rose in a cloudless sky and beat down as fiercely as the day before. It was, then, in Brive or Cahors, one evening after sunset, but still light from the great glow in the west, that I first experienced the walls where we walked radiating back in waves the heat they had absorbed during the day.

Night brought some relief, but not much. From time to time we slept, as best we could, in the car. Alan managed this without complaint, folding his bony body over the steering wheel with an appearance of comfort, from being used to it we supposed. For the rest of us, sleeping while sitting up in a confined space was a poor substitute for any kind of bed, though it made early rising a relief rather than a punishment to be borne. One night, after Brive or Cahors, Richie and I decided to sleep outside the car. We had a couple of khaki blankets, small and rough, ex-army kit, which Alan had packed. He had brought them for spreading on the ground when we ate al fresco, to avoid the expense of bars and brasseries. The car was parked on a grassy verge with all the windows wide. Alan and Gwyn had a little more space to stretch themselves while we took a blanket each, used the torch to find a likely looking patch nearby and settled.

The road was empty. Night sounds of insects were lulling rather than irritating and it was otherwise intensely still, not a breath of wind. No moon. We might have been the last humans on earth, lying on our backs, wrapped in warm, velvet blackness sprinkled with limitless glittering sparks of light, some in familiar patterns, shifting at a blink, but there, still there, eternally there, while the eyes remained open.

I don't know how long I lay gazing upwards and then perhaps sleeping, but I was awakened by a strange hiccuping sound. It took me a while to recognise it was suppressed sobbing a few feet away, where Richie lay.

'Richie, are you all right? What's the matter?'

My voice was little more than a whisper, but he heard. 'It's nothing,' he said. 'Go back to sleep.'

'Is there anything I can do?'

After a long pause – 'Don't you feel it – this enormous sky pressing down? And all those stars. What does it mean? All the emptiness and... spots of light. What are we doing here, on the edge of this terrible vacancy? What's the point of it all? I don't think I've ever felt so alone.'

'But I'm here – and Gwyn and Alan.'

'It's no comfort – human contact, because we're all in

the same boat. We can grasp one another, and even hold on for the moment of existence, but in the end, and very soon, we are, all of us, alone.'

I could think of nothing to say in the silence that followed. Then he began to speak again, less agonisingly than before.

'It's my imagination, my conscience – and this endless black going on and on, past the stars. Don't worry, I shall be all right.'

Having seemingly talked himself out of the depths, he fell silent and soon drifted off to sleep, while I lay awake, puzzled and disturbed by the strength of his feelings.

When I stirred, it was already light, with the promise of another day of sun and black shadows of trees on the road we would travel. The blanket, my clothes, my bare arms and face were wet with dew. Richie, smoking the stub of a cigarette, was roaming about the car where Alan and Gwyn were alert and talking together. I did not speak to Richie about what had occurred in the darkness, nor mention it to the others.

The next night, Gwyn and I shared the back seat of the car. Stirring out of sleep, I felt a nudge to attend. It had been a comfortless night. With the windows open, the constant riot of crickets from grass and bushes where we had parked was unbearable, their multitudinous scrapings merging into a continuous screech. Once closed, though the sound was muted, the windows quickly misted and it was stifling. At some point the crickets had had enough and we had all nodded off, and now it was grey dawn.

The nudge, more a poke, came again and I turned my stiff neck away from the seat corner and sweating window to look at Gwyn, who was tensely still and wide awake. The dim forms in front, both bent forward, Alan with head on arms folded over the steering wheel. Then I heard it: a strange whistling sound that seemed to move over the car – not a bird, deeper than the crickets' note – with a long slow trill. Silence again. At the third repetition Alan awoke with a start.

'Christ! Enemy fire. Out! Out!' he shouted, scrabbling for the handle and throwing himself through the car door.

I had never heard him curse or even raise his voice but, responding to his cry, struggled to open the door and fling myself onto the dew-drenched grass beside him. Gwyn came crawling around the back of the car and joined us. 'What is it?' he said.

Alan had regained his composure and got to his feet. 'I'm sorry – shouldn't have done that. One of those things. Didn't mean to alarm you. Reflex action.' And then, after a deep breath, 'Look at him.'

I could see Richie through the open driver's side door, eyes still closed, fumbling in his pockets. In a moment or so he had found and lit his first cigarette of the day. He stretched, rubbed a hand over his face, pushed his floppy dark hair back and put on his glasses. Seeing us together, he opened his door and came around to our side.

'Anyone making tea?' he said.

Two more prolonged whistles crossed above us in quick succession.

Richie glanced up, narrowing his eyes in the plume of cigarette smoke, 'Hello, sounds like bombs.'

'No, they're shells.' Alan was calm, his usual self. 'I think we parked in the middle of a firing range. Last night, in the dark, I didn't see a warning sign. Perhaps there isn't one. They've got artillery practice probably three or four miles off south of here and the target maybe another three or four, perhaps more, over there. Depends on the gun.' He pointed to the vague outlines of hills emerging from morning mist to the north. 'There's nothing to worry about. At least there shouldn't be. Shells do sometimes fall short, for all sorts of reasons, mostly carelessness, but it's pretty rare. All the same, it may be wiser to clear out of here. Can you wait for your tea, Richie?'

Thirty minutes later and well away from whistling shells, we sat at the roadside around our camping kettle. The morning mist was dissipating, but rising still like smoke over patches of dense woodland, and, though the steep upper reaches of the valley sides along the way we had come stood out crisp and bright in the new day's sun, it lay thick still over the curving course of a river at their foot. Perhaps that was the Tarn; I cannot be sure. Alan read the maps he had bought on previous trips and knew where we were going ('mostly down the N9'), while we just viewed the landscape as we passed.

Richie was feeding twigs and dry grass down the funnel of the camping kettle and withdrawing his hand quickly as flames licked out of the top. The contraption was new to me, but it worked. In a couple of minutes we would have boiling water for the aluminium teapot. It was Gwyn who, not looking at Alan, quietly, hesitantly, opened the topic.

'You know... you know all about... shellfire.'

In the silence that followed I could hear the hum of flames in the chimney of the kettle and the first rattle of water bubbling in the metal jacket. We knew Alan had served in the war, but he never talked about it, and if he didn't want to talk, it didn't seem right to ask. The momentary jarring experience, like suddenly waking into a nightmare, as it must have been for him, had lifted the embargo.

'Yes, I know about shellfire. I think I know the guns being fired this morning. There may be some new French artillery, but the chances are we heard shells from 105mm or 155mm howitzers, both good, reliable weapons, adopted by several other countries, including the States. The 155mm lobs a shell weighing almost a hundredweight about seven and a half miles. Yes, I know that the Germans captured a lot of them at the beginning of the war and used them against us in Normandy. The Vietminh have just captured more after over-running Dien Bien Phu last May.'

He looked around. We managed barely a nod of understanding between us. I had heard of Dien Bien Phu, had seen it in newspaper headlines, but I was politically naïve. Ignorant, rather. It meant very little to me.

'I think that probably means the end of French Indo-China,' Alan said, 'and I doubt the communists will stop there.'

This was a different Alan, not the cheerfully unassuming

companion of our travels, and more than the serious student of history Gwyn and Richie had befriended. We three had been children during the war, had traced or pasted anti-Nazi cartoons from the newspapers into scrapbooks, seen newsreels of the fighting in North Africa, Europe and the Pacific, saved to buy books describing campaigns, with little real understanding pored over battle maps with their snaking arrows and brutal, inspiring photographs of hard-fought victories they contained, the shattered towns, burned out tanks bearing the black Nazi cross on their turrets, dejected German prisoners, hands aloft or plodding in straggling columns under the guns of grimly smiling Tommies. (There were no photographs of British dead, wounded perhaps, smiling through pain, but not the dead.)

'Do you know how they did it?' Alan went on. 'It was an inspired piece of planning and sheer slog to stand with those celebrated in military history.'

Together we shook our heads.

'At Dien, the French had established a strong base in a valley surrounded by steep hills covered with dense jungle. They had an airstrip there, one the Japs had built during the last war, for food and arms to be flown in as required. The French general liked the look of the place, thought it was a good position to block communist routes into Laos. He didn't for one moment think the Vietminh would dismantle heavy guns and carry them in bits up the hills, through the jungle.' He looked down at his fine, long-fingered hands and spread his fingers. 'But they did just that, and then they reassembled them and dug them in overlooking the valley.'

I was mesmerised and could see Gwyn and Richie were listening intently.

'And when they were ready they blasted the airstrip and command centres in plain view below them. Because of the jungle the French couldn't get an accurate fix on where the shells were coming from. and their aircraft couldn't risk flying in with fresh supplies. They held out not much more than a month before surrendering.'

We drank our tea in silence, and Richie smoked another precious cigarette down to the last tenth of an inch, his hand cupped, the stub clamped between thumb and forefinger.

An hour or so later, thirty-odd miles down the road towards the Spanish border, the sun was well up and the last rags of mist had dispersed. It must have been still no more than seven o'clock – a glorious day, not yet hot, the car running through light and shade, the shadows of buildings and trees already black. We dawdled through villages scanning the main street for a boulangerie open for business and eventually spotted one. We bought a couple of baguettes. In those days you could rely on finding a stall or café-bar in most villages with a big bowl of hard-boiled eggs on the counter and a sign saying 'Oeufs à la coque'. They were very cheap and convenient eating. We had a few eggs and some soft cheese left over from the previous day, and butter packed in two jars, which Richie's mother insisted we take with us, that had become semi-solid again overnight. With pepper and salt and a couple of apples, and more tea, we had enough for breakfast.

I'd been thinking about what we had been told of the

fall of Dien Bien Phu and was curious about Alan's knowledge of that battle and familiarity with French artillery. He was something under average height, the shortest of us on that trip, and lean, not an ounce of fat, and hair brownish, thinning now, under a constant black beret. No matter what Richie and Gwyn told me, this gentle, soft-spoken man was not my idea of a soldier. I was chewing this over with breakfast and the question came out before I'd properly thought about it.

'How did you come to join up?'

There was a silence in which Richie and Gwyn looked uncomfortable, and Gwyn said, 'I wonder will we cross the border today.'

Alan looked at me. 'Well,' he said, shrugging, 'as soon as war was declared conscription started. If you were over 18, that was it. My eighteenth birthday was in January 1940, and I was lucky to be able to stay in school until I finished Higher Cert exams in June. I was medically fit, had no conscientious objection to fighting, especially when it came to Hitler and Nazism, and didn't have the prospect of the sort of job that made you more useful out of the army than in – what they called a "reserved occupation". So that was it.'

He may not have looked my idea of a soldier, but had little choice in the matter. Even then, nine years after it was all over, at nineteen, I would have been in the army, doing National Service, if I'd not made myself temporarily exempt by going to college. The same applied to Richie and Gwyn. And the army was poised to nab us as soon as we left college, if we didn't find our way into a "reserved occupation".

I wanted to ask Alan what it was like in the army, wanted to know more about where and how he had served, but Gwyn began to be ostentatiously busy packing up our breakfast things. I couldn't understand why he was so keen to interrupt the conversation since Alan didn't seem to mind, but we became busy too, and the chance was gone.

It was by accident we found ourselves in Llo. The initial problem may have arisen from misreading the map, though that is to suggest Alan made an error, which is exceedingly unlikely. He had been keen to give us a taste of the Pyrénées, where he, too, had not travelled before, having on previous trips roughly followed the British forces campaign trail from Normandy across the north of France and the Rhine. Perhaps that led him to choose a dog-leg route over the border rather than the more direct N 9 south of Perpignan down to Barcelona.

I remember we left the outskirts of Perpignan mid-afternoon heading south-west towards Pradès. It was quiet after the stir of traffic around the town, and out in the country there was only the occasional vehicle of any sort, even horse or mule-drawn. It was very hot and the air seemed crackling with drought as though on the edge of spontaneous combustion. The river alongside the road was reduced to a trickle wandering a broad stony bed, and we were heading in the general direction of its source. Richie and I, in the back seat, viewing the landscape to the south, saw lines of craggy mountains folded one beyond the other, peak rising above peak, blue in the distance and, surpassing all, one colossal domed summit.

'What's that mountain?' I said, 'Can't we stop?'

Alan brought the car to a halt and we got out. Gwyn fumbled with the map, following with his finger the line of our road. 'It must be Canigou. It says here 2,785 – that's metres.'

'Something over nine thousand feet,' Alan added. 'That's quite a sight. Worth stopping for. And not that far from the coast: its drop must be huge.'

I took the map from Gwyn and peered at it. 'Canigou,' I said, 'I see – Canigou.'

'Here let me fold it.' Alan's voice betrayed barely a hint of irritation. 'Treat them with respect, I was told. They may save your life.'

We gazed at Canigou with its attendant peaks, the sun still high but westering, and a great slash of purple cloud, like a bruised and bleeding gash across the pale blue to the south. From a distance of about twenty miles, to those accustomed to the petty mountains of south Wales, it was magnificent.

In the car once more, above the noise of the engine and the air rushing under the lifted windscreen, Alan told us about the far higher peaks of eastern France and Switzerland, many over four thousand metres. Once, he said, he had stopped overnight at a run-down chalet hotel, the only guest, in a village called Megéve, near Mont Blanc, the highest of the lot, and had the tremendous view of snow-capped peaks all around at the height of summer.

'I'd like to climb there,' said Richie.

'You'd risk your life like that?' Gwyn called back without turning his head.

'Yes,' said Richie, and he laughed, 'it's risky ... but what a way to go!'

Soon after this interlude, we turned into the foothills and onto a narrow road that rose sharply in a succession of tight bends. The air was suddenly chilly. Alan took over the driving, closed the windscreen and was busy at the wheel as we climbed loop after loop. We swayed to the motion of the car and conversation lapsed. As though a curtain had been drawn, with one dramatic gesture the sky darkened and it started to rain. At first we thought a summer shower will be refreshing and the parched land needs this, but a flash lit the road ahead and the interior of the car with blinding white light. In that split second Richie's face, leaning close to me, was deathly pale, his lips stretched in a grin. He was enjoying what others might have thought a glimpse of Armageddon. An enormous thunderclap overhead was accompanied by rain of such intensity that the barrage of drops on the car roof made speaking impossible and the windscreen wipers couldn't cope.

We could see nothing in the blurred darkness beyond the few yards straight ahead barely lit by the headlights, but I sensed we had reached the top of the climb when the angle of the car and the tone of the engine changed together, and then, still in loops, we were going down. Alan was peering ahead, concentrating on keeping the wheels on the narrow road as we veered between rock walls that loomed on one side and an unguarded clifftop edge on the other. In the end the car skidded sideways as Alan braked, somehow eased itself beneath a slight overhang and slithered to a stop.

Alan gasped aloud and after a pause drew breath and spoke slowly against the roll of the storm drumming on the roof above our heads with myriad fingers. 'I think we're safe here for a while. Nothing else moving on this road – thank goodness. I can't see where we're going, so it's pointless and probably dangerous trying to struggle on.'

With the engine dead, we could hear run-off flowing around the wheels in torrents, but the car stood still in the swirling water

'A nice little bulge of rock,' said Richie, rubbing the misted window and peering up. 'The forehead of a mountain god. I wouldn't mind having a go at that. With all the water streaming down you can't see, but I bet there are hand and footholds enough to get up and over.'

Gwyn was unhappy about our predicament and a little breathless. 'You must be mad. We'll be lucky if the rain doesn't wash down mud and rocks from above, if not send the whole lot crashing on top of us.'

Richie reached out and gripped my knee. I turned and saw the gleam of his teeth through the gloom. He was smiling. 'With that precipice, it would be over in a flash,' he said. 'No point in worrying.'

Late afternoon was dark as night. We waited, hardly speaking, as the deluge continued. When at last it slackened we slowly moved on, downstream it seemed. In the gloom, with the windscreen wipers doing their best, we somehow missed our way and turned into a road that, at first, looked so much like the other we were not alerted to the deviation. The way ahead gradually narrowed to the width of a single vehicle and the surface became rugged. We lurched along, the rain again falling heavily, until we glimpsed through the murk a dark building. At first we thought it must be a house, where we might knock on the door, ask directions and hope for a hospitable welcome, but it showed no glimmer of light and, when at last the headlights swung fully onto it, we saw it was a barn and that the big door was open. Alan said nothing but drove straight in. The beating on the car roof stopped as though switched off. When the engine died we got out stiffly and stood looking at one another, hushed by the falling rain beyond the open door.

The still darkness of the barn came as a relief. With the aid of the torch, Alan lit the hurricane lamp, unused until that moment, and held it up. The building was soundly roofed, no sign of water dripping inside and as the light increased it revealed some heaps of straw and hay roughly baled.

'There are probably rats,' said Gwyn, 'and I know it's early, but I'm going to have a rest.'

He flung himself onto the nearest bundle of straw and closed his eyes.

We were under cover, for which we were grateful, but tired and lost and a long way from home. Torrential rain, the winding road, had taken a toll on nerves. Anticipating the heat of the day and the usual balmy evening, we were lightly clothed. The chill that comes with a storm in the mountains was a shock. I shivered as I sank into a scooped nest of straw. Alan hung the lamp on a convenient nail, kicked together clumps of straw into a mound and settled into it.

Richie, a little distance off in his own nest, was humming to himself. 'Could do with a cigarette,' he said.

'Not here,' said Alan.

'Very well, I'll suck a straw.'

I could tell he was still, unaccountably, in a good humour.

From quite near on my left, Alan said, almost to himself, 'No point in attempting to press on. We'll see where we are in the morning.'

The hurricane lamp had gone out. 'Is this what you'd call a bivouac?' I said to the darkness.

After a pause Alan answered quietly, 'No – not really. A bivouac is a sort of temporary stop, outdoors, without cover. And this barn is beginning to feel rather snug.'

'I expect soldiers get separated and lost on campaign?'

Another, longer pause. Then, 'Yes, from time to time, under bombardment, or when you're moving forward, or retreating for that matter. Or one or two simply stop, for whatever reason, and get left behind. All sorts of things... It's the job of the company commander and platoon commanders under him to keep an eye open for such eventualities. Action can be confusing, very confusing; you've got to keep a clear head. And a lot depends on planning. You need to know... exactly... what you're aiming to do.'

He was talking quietly, and I listened intently. There were no sounds of movement from the other piles of straw. Whether Gwyn and Richie were asleep, or feigning sleep, I couldn't tell.

'You saw a lot... I mean you were in the fighting?'

'Well, yes. It's not the sort of thing I care to think about.'

I stammered apologies, offering as excuse the information I had not previously shared with anyone at college, that my uncle, my mother's older brother, a marine, had not returned from the Dieppe raid. I remembered the strange quiet that lingered in the house for some time after we were told about the official telegram to his wife. It affected my mother painfully, but I had felt no sense of grief – I hope because I was too young to fully understand what "missing, believed killed" meant, rather than that I was devoid of feeling.

To my surprise, after a pause Alan continued, quietly as before. I hear now that soft voice in the still darkness, punctuated only by a slow drip from the roof of the barn on the wet earth beneath heard through the open door. It was as though he had been holding down the lid of a box, but it had tilted open despite his efforts, and now there seemed little point in trying to reseal it. He told how his basic training had been in the infantry, with the Welsh Fusiliers, how his knowledge of French had led to transfer to army intelligence and specialist training. In 1944 he found himself promoted lieutenant back in the 53rd Welsh Infantry Division for the north-west Europe campaign, from Normandy to the surrender of the German army at Lüneberg Heath.

'In the war,' he said, 'you are blinkered – if you are lucky. You can see only immediate responsibilities and challenges. And that's good: it's what keeps you sane. Concentrating absolutely on what must be done, with the men under your command ... shuts out everything else. You see dreadful things, but somehow they don't register, not at the time, because your mind is so fixed on ... *what must be done*, with and for them. When you lose one of them it is – terrible.'

After a long pause, 'And then you concentrate again.'

He told of briefing meetings at which he accompanied his company commander, where General Dempsey, who led the British Second Army, demonstrated his extraordinary ability at interpreting battlefield maps and planning combined operations. Dempsey had been a First World War hero and in the Second he was a master of strategy.

'He'd look at a map, you know, and I'd swear he could *see* the terrain.'

I heard the emotion choking Alan's voice as he spoke of him, and again a pause.

'At the crossing of the Rhine the plan was to mount a two-pronged attack, near a town called Wesel, one directly across the river, the other airborne, a little farther east, using parachute drops and gliders.'

It had all kicked off in the third week of March 1945, very early in the morning, a moonless sky lit by flashes of gunfire and the fiery glare of explosions beyond the opposite bank of the river. They were waiting for signals when the company commander and two others at a forward post on the river bank were hit by a mortar and killed.

'I got in touch with brigade. I don't know whether it went further up the line, but anyway, since I had been present at the general's briefing and was the next senior officer on the ground, I was told to take command, nominally as major, until there was time to sort things out.'

The bridges had all been destroyed. His company, about two hundred men, used amphibious vehicles to cross the river, got themselves dug in under fire on the other side and the next day slowly pushed forward. Wesel itself was flattened by earlier bombing and a long artillery barrage on the morning of the attack.

'As soon as our forces had established a position on the other bank, work began on a pontoon bridge. So we crossed the Rhine and transport and heavy weapons followed pretty quickly. Things went more or less according to plan ... It didn't take long for a new company commander to take over and then we pressed on through Bremen, and Hamburg – and Kiel. It was a bit stiff going at the start and in odd pockets, but most of the Wehrmacht had had enough ... ashen-faced prisoners in droves, many sullen, some failing to hide their relief, quite a number little more than schoolboys. You would see these places on the map, the next objective and so on, but when you got there it was always the same ... endless destruction and ruin, and desperate people. I told myself I would go back when the war was over ... just to see what happened to it all ... and I've done that.'

I heard him settle deeper in the straw and soon his breathing told me he was asleep. Still no sound from Richie and Gwyn, but perhaps they had been listening, too. I lay wakeful for a long time turning over what Alan had said. How could a skinny, sensitive, clever fellow have put up with it, and survived? Heroes, in my imagination, were big, brawny men with an air of bravado, and Alan was the antithesis of that. If he'd won a medal or been mentioned in dispatches, he didn't say, and I decided I wouldn't press him any more.

The rain had stopped when we stirred. It was not long past first light. I remember stretching and stepping outside the barn into an immense stillness, no breath of wind, and silence apart from the sounds of water oozing and dripping. Chilled by the clear mountain air, we hunted out sweaters and fragments of food, and took the kettle outside to brew-up. There was no shortage of dry stuff in the barn for burning and outside water lay all around in large puddles.

'Don't worry, we're boiling it,' said Alan, as Gwyn raised objections, and Richie, slapping his arms briskly to get the circulation going, laughed.

We saw that the barn was strangely isolated, no farm nearby, no other building in sight. After tea and a few biscuits from a pack Richie's mother had pressed on him as he was setting out, neglected until this hour of need, we returned to the car. There was light enough now inside the barn from a window in the eastern wall, beyond which the sun was rising. It was a sizeable, arched window, unglazed but vertically striped with wooden bars. Several narrow patches of paler light in the other walls were slots designed, we thought, to allow air to circulate. It was a remarkably stout building for storing hay and straw, the stone walls thick enough to withstand a siege, the steeply pitched roof supported by massive beams.

'I'm not sure this was meant to be a barn,' Gwyn said. 'Perhaps it started out as a house – or a chapel.'

'Or a fortification, part of an outlying defensive position. But defending what?' We looked around the interior again and could see sense in Alan's suggestion.

Richie was staring into the roof space. He took off his glasses, rubbed them on the tail of his shirt and adjusted them to peer up again. 'There's bats,' he said.

We all looked up and, sure enough, flickering shadows were dodging among the beams. 'No, I don't think they're bats. Look – they're coming through the window.'

Gwyn was right. Birds were slicing through the window slats and fluttering to nests like brown blisters stuck here and there to the beams. The speed of their entry through the narrow gaps was breathtaking. As we watched we became aware of faint twitterings as the parent birds returned.

'Ah, breakfast time,' said Richie. 'What are they?'

'Swifts.' Gwyn was confident. 'They're hunting insects and bringing them back for the nestlings.'

Alan was turning away. 'Let's get back on the road, find something to eat, and sort out the route. Once is enough to be lost in the mountains.'

I could have stayed longer, watching the shadows that filled the western side of the barn gradually yield to day. Outside, water filling every depression glinted silver like spilled mercury. Swifts circled with shrill cries, swooping in turn to unzip the larger pools and flashing away again in the strengthening sun. And we, too, were hungry and thirsty. Despite the drenching journey, the car started without trouble. The high crests were already well alight when we left our shelter and drove back along the track, slick with mud, to the fork in the road where we had gone wrong the previous night. Half a mile farther on we saw the sign: 'Llo'.

Apart from their straight trajectory to the next

destination, one of the things I learned to like about French roads on that trip is that you know at once when you enter a town or village and, with the same sign cancelled, the moment you leave it. But this was the strangest place-name we encountered on the journey and we wondered how it was said. Did the first two letters make the single sound 'L'? Or was it a Spanish double-L, which Alan assured us was pronounced like 'Y' in English.

Richie was adamant the villagers were a lost tribe from Wales marooned in the valley by bad weather centuries ago and the 'Ll' came naturally to them. He volunteered to act as interpreter and began polishing up the few Welsh phrases he possessed. Then he changed his mind. 'It's a misprint for "LO",' he said, 'a greeting to anyone daft enough to take the wrong road, as we did, and of course they're French, so they've lost the aspirate. "Hello!" or "Ello" – friendly like.'

But there were no friendly greetings. The place seemed deserted. It was still early, but we expected to see someone on the road or in a field. And where was the usual village street with its boulangerie, épicerie and café-bar? So far as we could tell, this place in the mountains didn't have a main street. The road ended abruptly. Alan pulled up and we gathered outside the car to look about. There was a ruin poised on a crag, castle or possibly convent, a battered tower on another rocky eminence, scattered dwellings, and fenced or walled fields on a steep valley side with unsurfaced paths wandering among them, some only a foot or so wide others a yard or two. It was so quiet in the early morning air that we spoke low, almost in whispers, as we discussed which way to go. Smoke rising from chimneys suggested food was being prepared, but there were no people to be seen. The houses of stone and wood with their small windows looked ancient. We seemed to have entered another world, remote, medieval.

'There must be a boulangerie,' said Alan. 'I have never been in a French village without one – even during the war. We'll have to ask at a house.'

We started along one of the broader paths and soon came upon a wooden shed. A glazed window on a side wall revealed it was packed with hay.

'Strange. Have you ever seen hay stored in a shed?' Richie, gazing through the window, was bemused.

'Perhaps it's because of the rain,' Gwyn said. 'If it had been out last night, it would have been ruined.'

'But you put hay in a barn. A shed-full wouldn't last a day. Whoa! There's something moving in there. Look.'

We gathered around the small, grimy pane. There was, as Richie had seen, movement inside. Shortly, a rabbit conjured itself out of the hay and looked at us.

'That's a surprise,' I said. 'Has it burrowed in from underneath?'

Another rabbit came into view. 'I think it's someone's meat larder,' said Alan. 'If you fancy a rabbit for the pot, you don't go out with a gun hoping to bag one, you go down the shed and take your pick.'

But there was no sign of anyone wanting one for the pot that morning: the locals seemed in no hurry to begin the day. We agreed the only solution was to knock someone's door. The house nearest the rabbit shed appeared much like the barn that had afforded us shelter during the stormy night– the same steeply-pitched roof of thick stone tiles, the same stout walls – though considerably smaller and with a low extension, at the farther end of which a squat chimney smoked.

Alan volunteered to do the talking. Our dumb presence behind him may have appeared threatening to the man who answered his knock. As though our approach had been observed, the door opened at once, but a few inches only, so that we caught a glimpse of a rough-hewn, unshaven face for a second before it closed again smartly with a bang.

'No luck there, then,' said Richie.

'And no point in knocking again – let's try the next.'

The path skirted a rocky outcrop and, rounding it, some fifty yards off, we saw another dwelling much like the first, but with a fenced yard in front, where a woman dressed entirely in voluminous black was scattering scraps from a bowl for a small flock of chickens. Two chickens hung by the legs from a short line between two poles, flapping their wings in a desultory way. The woman was bent and white-haired and so occupied with her task and the clucking fowls she didn't notice our approach. She inverted the bowl and tapped the bottom to empty it, then turning to the chickens hanging on the line, took a knife from her apron pocket and neatly cut their throats one after the other. The dark blood streamed down as the birds flapped a few times and were still.

'My God,' said Richie, 'that was neat.'

Gwyn shook his head. 'I didn't expect that,' he said. 'Let's go somewhere else.'

But Alan was already approaching the fence. We stood some distance off, while, beret in hand, he greeted her. The woman did not run back into the house, as we half expected, but came to the gate in the fence. There was conversation, of which we heard only a murmuring, and then she disappeared indoors while Alan waited. In a few minutes she returned, handing over a package.

'She wouldn't take any money for this,' sad Alan unwrapping a few roughly hacked slices of stale bread, a shapeless lump of hard cheese and half-a-dozen small green apples.'

Richie laughed. 'It was probably food for the chickens. A short life but full of good things.'

'We've seen what you meant about the rabbits,' Gwyn said. 'I don't think it entirely puts me off meat, though a warning before the butchery started would have been appreciated.'

'I'd rather a chicken leg than what she's given us.'

'It's meant to tide us over. Apparently there's a good spring farther up the mountain, if we need a drink. She told me there is no boulangerie, but bread is delivered daily about ten o'clock to a bar near the church, where orders can be placed. That won't help us, of course. The bread comes from Bourg-Madame about ten kilometres off.'

Gwyn saw no point in hanging about, when we could go on to Bourg-Madame, wherever that was, find the baker's, or a café – buy some breakfast. The idea made him suddenly cheerful.

Alan unfolded his map. 'Yes,' he said, 'I can see now where we went wrong last night. It means retracing our route a bit, but not very far at all, and then the road via Bourg-Madame, the N116, will take us to Barcelona – about a hundred miles.'

'Since we're here,' said Richie, 'can't we get up the mountain a bit – not far – just to see the view? It's not exactly welcoming, but I rather like Llo. You must admit it's a bit unusual.'

He chose the Welsh pronunciation and, head held high, right arm extended at shoulder height, mimed a dance, intoning 'Llo, Llo, quick, quick, Llo' in the manner of Victor Sylvester.

We overcame Gwyn's protest and set off on a broad path, sunk below the level of the surrounding grassy slope, which led diagonally up the mountain's flank. It had been battered by the passage of countless animals, deeper hoofprints silvered by last night's rain, the sort of beaten track created over decades, even centuries, by herds moving to and fro between low and high pastures as the seasons turned. The valley behind was warming and drying in bright morning sun, the sky an immense, immaculate blue. Flowers flourished on the banks either side and spread out over the grass and among the rocks beyond.

We found the spring, gushing after the heavy rain, in a casing of stone slabs, and opened the pack of food. The stale bread had the texture and taste of cardboard, the local cheese, hard for long keeping, but kept too long, was equally resistant to chewing and flavourless, the apples were unripe and bitter.

'A nice little treat,' said Gwyn. 'I doubt the hens would have made much of it.'

Alan sawed the bread and cheese into bite-sized lumps

with his penknife. 'It's a good deal more than a lot of people had in northern France and Germany not too long ago,' he said. 'If you were really hungry you'd eat this – and far worse than this.'

We were hungry, and a little chastened, so we took the proffered fragments and chewed vigorously, bit into the sharp apples, and cupped our hands to the icy water for drink.

At the top of the first rise we turned to view the way we had come.

'Llo and behold,' said Richie, again Welshifying the consonant and gesturing towards the village below.

It had an aura of antiquity. People were beginning to move along the trails, but no sounds apart from occasional birdsong and the braying of a donkey rose up to us, and there was no sign of farm machinery, or vehicles of any kind, apart from the black carapace of our Morris at the end of the track where we had left it. The broken tower on the other side of the valley stood in isolation but several houses and smaller buildings were gathered directly below us, near the castle on its rocky plinth, and there, too, was the church, though larger, much like the houses from a distance, except for its belcote, where there seemed to be two bells. The promised bar would be nearby.

The path continued, rather more gently, to an area of what appeared rough pasture, a tableland spreading several hundred yards to the foot of another much steeper rise. At this level there were fewer flowers, but the coarse grass was alive with grasshoppers and the air filled with their chirpings as the sun's light intensified and its warmth spread. There, too, we came upon a wire strung on metal pegs, about a foot high, driven into the ground, and extending into the distance.

'What's that for?' said Gwyn. 'Is it electrical? It's not going to keep animals in – or out.'

Richie and I were equally puzzled, but Alan laughed: 'No – though *you* are not supposed to cross it without your passport. It's the border. Step over and you're in Spain.

It was irresistible. 'There we are – I've been to Spain. Shall we go home now?' I could tell from his tone Gwyn had not spoken entirely in jest, and silently admitted to myself that, if at a click of my fingers I could be back, I would probably have done just that. It was homesickness, I thought, but not a continuing dull ache as the term seemed to imply, rather a sharp unexpected pang, a sudden realisation that home was very far away. The other two had already turned and were making their way to the path, Richie gesticulating and speaking animatedly, while Alan nodded.

In another hour or so we were in Bourg Madame, where an ordinary breakfast of coffee and croissants was a memorable feast. Oil checked, petrol tank filled, the car was ready for the road. In another hour we had come down from the mountains and, after a short delay at the frontier where visas were inspected and solemn customs officials looked over the car, we were in Spain, heading south on the coastal road towards Barcelona.

The two photographs, one of an almost vertical pale cliff towering over a narrow road and the other of diminutive figures looking upwards at a shattered viaduct, were almost certainly taken on the Spanish side of the Pyrénées at a stop on the road between Bourg-Madame and the Mediterranean coast. I don't recall the occasion; it was, after all, more than sixty years ago. I do remember the first real sight of the sunstruck sea stretching away to our left as we journeyed south. I have looked out over the Med from promenades and beaches in France, Spain and Italy many times since, and what impressions I have of its variegated colours, dark and light blues and greens, turquoise, the deepest purple, have been gathered more recently (and supplemented by tourist-luring photographs), but nothing has matched the enchantment of that first long look as the Morris travelled the rutted and potholed N11 towards Barcelona. There was very little traffic. But every now and then as we neared villages we would pass mule-drawn wagons, rather like much smaller versions of the prairie schooners we used to see in cowboy films, and donkeys with hugely loaded panniers on either side and often a woman or a small boy with a stick urging them onward.

Alan remembered hearing and reading about the Civil War in Spain, but it had meant little to him at the time. He had learned a great deal more since his own involvement in the conflict with fascist Germany. Barcelona, where we were heading, was vehemently anti-fascist. He told Richie and me, if we fancied ourselves as students of English literature, we ought to have read Orwell's *Homage to Catalonia*. When the topic came up as we were bumping along the coast road, I had to admit I had not.

'Look, we've had exams,' Richie said, 'no time for stuff outside the syllabus. But I will read it –promise.'

'A bit late now. One thing you'd all better remember – be careful what you say about Franco.'

'I'll be sure to smile when I mention the name.'

'Franco – fascist bastard,' said Richie, smiling broadly.

'It's not a joke,' said Alan. 'You never know who might be listening, taking note of strangers – what they did, what they said – and passing it on to the authorities. That's the way fascist governments keep an eye on things, keep everyone in order. Communists likewise.'

Richie still smiled, though rather sheepishly. 'OK,' I said, 'message received and understood.'

Alan hadn't finished. He did not have to fabricate his dislike and distrust of Franco. He had good reason to curse him to hell. 'He's the last of the fascist dictators in our part of the world. Without the help of his allies, Hitler and Mussolini, he would not have won the civil war. Hitler used Spain for a trial run of his blitzkrieg strategy – bombing unarmed, unprotected citizens. Most of the brightest and best of Spain were lined up against Franco, and they did have Russian support, as you would know, if you'd read Orwell, but it was nothing compared to the active involvement of Nazi Germany and Fascist Italy.'

We stopped at El Masnou, a small town on the coast about a dozen miles short of Barcelona, where a bed and food would be less expensive. There we found a pension, or *fonda*, the Comodoro, where full board was sixty pesetas. That I remember well, because the peseta was worth about tuppence, and it meant we would each have a room and all meals for ten shillings a day. Alan had told us living would be cheaper in Spain, but this was better than we had dared hope. The hotel shared an off-road parking area with a garage where we could buy petrol and three or four young men had a vehicle repair shop. They clustered about the Morris inspecting engine and controls. There was little traffic of any sort and they seemed to think it was a particular mark of favour to have a foreign vehicle on their forecourt. Ours were the only foreign voices in the hotel. Our lack of Spanish was a handicap, and Alan's French was often greeted with incomprehension, but our attempts at communication were received with patience and misunderstandings on both sides which usually ended in laughter.

It was Hemingway who began my interest in American literature. He, too, above all others, persuaded me to join Alan's expedition to Spain. I was still in school when I first read about him in the pages of *Picture Post*, which ran an illustrated account of him surviving a plane crash while big game hunting. In the days when the idea of hunting lion or buffalo still seemed a great adventure to young males of a bookish disposition, I became fascinated by this writer who risked his life on the plains of Africa. Our local library had one of his books – *A Farewell to Arms*. I read it and asked for more. In due course they produced *Death in the Afternoon,* and I was hooked. It was inevitable the gaudy posters advertising bullfights in Barcelona on the walls of the bar in the hotel and elsewhere around the streets of El Masnou held a magnetic attraction for me. I had talked about bullfighting with Richie and knew he was interested, and Alan was intrigued enough to say he'd drive us into the city. Gwyn said he had doubts about the morality of it all and in the end preferred to stay about the hotel and the beach. He told us he would take a walk and write a letter. Nothing was said, but we knew he was thinking of Evelyn.

The bullfight was on a Sunday. On our way into Barcelona, we saw one of the lads from the garage, who had been admiring the Morris, at the side of the road. He was trying to thumb a lift. We had a spare seat, and no one objected to picking him up. Having thanked us, he went on in broken French and scant English to warn us never to stop for hitch-hikers. It was dangerous, he said. There were bad men, with guns, who rob rich people and steal their cars. We laughed at this.

'Why you laugh?' he said. *'Peligroso! Es importante!'*

We tried to explain that we were students – 'No money – old car', but he was very insistent, *'Peligroso!'*. In a little while he became reconciled to our foolhardiness and we managed to convey we were on our way to the bullfight. It was his turn to smile: *'Muy bien! Soy afortunado.'*

We were lucky, too. He was going to the bullfight and would guide us. Without his help we might have wandered the city for hours. *'Plaza de toros La Monumental,'* he declared as we approached what I recall now as a vast terracotta brick circular wall with towers at intervals crowned with white domes and decorated Moorish style with blue and white tiles, rather beautiful under a blue sky foaming with clouds. Our friend directed us to cheaper seats about halfway up a segment of *'sol y sombra'*, sun and shade. That day the sun was not blindingly hot and we were content to sit in it until its passage across the sky brought us into the shade. Once he was sure we were settled, he went off to join friends, like him regulars there.

From Hemingway I had learned that August bullfights in Barcelona were *novilladas*, which meant neither fighters nor bulls were of the best, and in turn accounted for surprisingly low admission prices. We were pleased about that. The fighters, *toreros*, were hoping to put on the kind of display that would help them on their way towards future fame and fortune. The bulls had no hope. They were there because they were too young or too old, or too big, for selection in top class *corridas*. Or they had been identified at the breeding farms as unreliable in their behaviour. In *novilladas*, I had read, a matador past his best, or a tyro still learning the trade might find himself pitted against an unpredictably dangerous beast. It was not simply a freak of chance that most of the deaths of bullfighters occurred in *novilladas*.

Such was my addiction to Hemingway at the time that knowing this had not blunted my desire to witness a *corrida*, but I could see momentary doubt crossing the minds of Alan and Richie, and Gwyn in particular, when I told them about it.

None of the *toreros* on the afternoon we witnessed was killed or, I think, looking back, suffered more than bruising about the ribs. After the mounted picadors had done their bit to weaken the bulls' prodigious neck muscles, all the horses left the ring on their own shod hooves. Only the bulls died, *pic*-ed by the lance, pierced by *banderillas,* blood streaming down their flanks, tormented, enraged, sacrificing themselves in a final charge onto the blade. The price of a deficit in skill on the part of the matador was prolongation of the suffering of the bull. How the crowd whistled and bawled their dissatisfaction with the performance. We saw one bullfighter, failing to deliver the *coup de grace* over the horns of the bull, caught on the creature's broad forehead, the horns either side of his narrow body, and the bull by that time too enfeebled even to push him over. Another lined up the bull, sword poised at arm's length, went in over the horns in the style demanded, and the blade, striking bone, bent double from the bull's surge and the tensile strength of the metal, sprang ten feet or more into the air, turning and glittering in the sun, before falling to the sanded floor of the arena. Three times he tried, three times, before he found the right spot and the bull impaled itself, and in a few strides more collapsed to its knees.

The *corrida* is a colourful spectacle, and noisy, with a band and the crowd engaged, as raucous in appreciation of a torero's daring and balletic grace, as they are in condemnation of a clumsy or cowardly performer. For all my enthusiasm before the event, having witnessed one, I had no wish to do so again. I wondered whether Richie with his hunger for risk had discovered a liking for it, could see himself as a future *afficionado,* but he, too, did not seem that impressed.

'Bloodier than I had imagined,' he said. 'I rather like the idea of facing the bull, drawing him to you with the cape and standing dead still as he sweeps by like an express train, the great horned head lifting to toss you skywards from the spot where he last fixed his eye on the target. It must be an extraordinary thrill deliberately to place yourself so close to death. Yes, I can see the attraction in that, for the bullfighter and the crowd. I didn't think the bulls would be that bloody big. They are huge – and beautiful. Did you see the way they entered the ring? Peering round with such fierce pride? "Who fancies his chances? Who's going to take me on?" Without the picador and the *banderilleros,* a dozen puny men, or more, wouldn't have a hope. It's not a fair fight is it? I didn't want to see a noble creature like that die and be hauled off without dignity – so much dead meat.'

'I told you we wouldn't be seeing bullfighting at its best,' I said, by way of self-justification, but I agreed with him. And he was right about the bull. I have never forgotten the excitement of its first entry into the ring. Hemingway had told me a lot about the fighting bull, but I was unprepared for such magnificence. He is black and huge, and comes in at a fast trot, head high, great horns aloft, an immense bulge of muscle at the shoulders, the base of the neck, and looks sharply about for anything disputing his space. He is god-like: it is easy to understand how he could be deified. At the end, the carcass is dragged out of the ring by a team of horses, the trail of blood he leaves swept into the sand. While you are yet considering the tragedy of his demise, the gate opens and the great black bull enters the ring at a smart trot, head high, horns aloft, a parable of resurrection.

We gave Gwyn our mixed review of the bullfight when we got back to the hotel. 'I don't think I missed much, then,' he said. He'd had a good time exploring the town, found shops where he'd bought postcards, and some splendid houses. El Masnou was not all about the sea-front. There was a prosperous quarter backing onto a park-like area of woodland and grassy clearings. He had finished and posted cards and a letter, sunbathed a while on the almost deserted beach, and paddled along the sea's edge. He was in a good mood.

For a few pennies, travel-stained clothes had been washed and ironed and returned to our rooms. When we went down to the bar we looked fresh and neatly pressed, and Gwyn's aura of contentment lifted us all. As a non-smoker, I was given custody of the dark blue box of fifty Player's. These precious fags from 'Duty Free' were meant to be reserved for such occasions and I had strict instructions to allow one each only when all three wanted a smoke. 'Make it last,' Gwyn said to Richie at the first distribution.

Red wine was less than tuppence a bottle; we bought two. It was slightly more palatable than the French wine we had met, and I decided to cultivate a taste for it. A glass or two was more than enough for the others and at Gwyn's instigation they had a glass of the Spanish brandy we had seen advertised with a bullfight image on roadside hoardings, 'Fundador Domecq'. A bottle of cointreau on a bar shelf caught Alan's eye. His recommendation accepted and swiftly endorsed, they settled to drinking alternately brandy and cointreau.

The bar slowly filled and became cheerfully noisy. This

was not the wealthier, refined part of El Masnou. Our guide to La Monumental turned up and introduced his friends from the garage. More brandy and cointreau appeared.

'How about a cigarette?' said Richie. 'I'm gasping.'

There were nods from the others and I proffered the dark-blue box. Interested and envious looks passed over the faces of the group of local men gathered at the bar as he, Alan and Gwyn lit up and puffed the smoke towards the beamed ceiling.

'God, that's better than the stuff in French fags.' As usual Richie had finished first. 'I rather like brandy and a Player's.'

One of the young men from the garage came over offering his own cigarettes. Alan and Gwyn shook their heads, indicating they were still smoking, but Richie accepted. *'Gracias,'* he said. 'Thank you. Very kind.'

The cigarette was a somewhat thicker tube than Player's, but the tobacco was loosely packed, and the paper, twisted at one end, flared up when it was lit.

'Thought you'd need an extinguisher,' said Gwyn. 'Be careful with the brandy. The whole lot could go up. What's it like anyway?'

'Awful. Why don't we give them a taste of a proper fag?'

'Yes, why not.' Gwyn said. 'What d'you think, Alan?'

Alan placed his empty brandy glass carefully on the tile-topped table. 'If that's what you want. See who'd like one.'

I got up and held out the open box. With exaggerated grace and many expressions of gratitude every man in the bar took a cigarette, looked at it carefully, rolled it in his fingers, smelled it, nodded approvingly to his neighbour, lit and inhaled deeply. As the smoke rose about them, they stood in relaxed, sophisticated attitudes and murmured to one another, *'Que es un buen cigarillo ... muy fino ... excelente.'*

Richie joined the group at the bar, there was much conversation, rapid-fire Spanish and exaggeratedly slow English, accompanied by signs and gestures, and a great deal of laughter. More drinks were ordered and glasses clinked: *'Salud!'*

Some time later, music was playing from an antique gramophone and Richie was dancing a Welsh flamenco with a plump cook, who, arms akimbo, flashed her eyes and rapped the floor with her heels. Everyone shouted and applauded, and Richie took the woman in his arms and clasped her tight until, flushed, she thrust him away so that he staggered and only saved himself from falling by grabbing the bar. He stood there spreading his arms in a gesture of innocence, before returning to our table grinning foolishly.

At Alan's suggestion we went outside for a breath of air. Gwyn said, 'I was looking at postcards of the Costa Brava earlier. They're in all the shops. It's beautiful – white houses, broad beaches, glorious sea colours. It would be great to go there.'

'Why not,' said Alan, smiling, pointing to the car. 'Here's the keys.'

'I'll drive,' said Richie. We all laughed.

'No – I'll drive,' he repeated. 'Alan, you show me.'

He took the keys and sat behind the wheel, Alan

alongside him. Gwyn and I climbed in the back, in time to hear Alan begin the instruction routine. 'Start the engine – left foot down on the clutch, all the way – gear lever into first – not there – no, there, that's right. Now right foot a touch on the accelerator, just a touch, and lift the left foot off the clutch slowly – handbrake off. Yes ...'

With a bound like a startled animal the car lurched forward a yard or two and stalled. Gwyn and I rolled in the back, helpless with laughter. Alan remained serious and calm. 'That's all right. We'll give it another try.'

He repeated the instruction, the car made another leap, and stalled.

'Perhaps we'd better put the headlights on before we try again.'

A small band of interested spectators, emerged from the bar, were rocking and clutching their sides. The night was balmy. A half-moon had slid over the roofs of the beach-side properties leaving a long trail of white light on the motionless sea; a host of stars glittered.

Richie wiped his glasses with a newly laundered handkerchief, settled them on his nose and peered ahead through the windscreen. He addressed himself to the controls again. 'I think I'm getting the hang of it,' he said. 'Foot down on the clutch, gear into first – a touch on the accelerator... foot slowly... off the clutch, handbrake off.'

The car jerked, moved forward a few yards and stopped.

'I'll do it if it kills me,' said Richie, amid breathless hoots and, indeed, at the next attempt succeeded in putting the Morris noisily in motion in first gear, turned left at the end of the forecourt and at a sharp reminder from Alan manoeuvred to the right hand side of the steeply-cambered road.

The night was suffused with the dim lights of moon and stars, but apart from those stationed at corners, there were no streetlights. Hunched forward, nose inches from the windscreen, Richie clung to the wheel as to a lifebelt in a storm at sea. The road ahead was mercifully straight and devoid of traffic.

We had travelled about half a mile and Gwyn was impressed. 'You've done it,' he said. 'I didn't think you were going to, but you have. What about changing gear? We're not going to get to the Costa Brava at this rate.'

Richie didn't lift his eyes as, grinding along in first, we slowly passed a pair of Guardia Civil armed with automatic weapons patrolling on either side of the road. They looked at the car curiously as it slowly passed them.

'Ahem,' said Alan, '– perhaps we'd better have a change of driver in case someone wants to see your licence. Do you know how to stop?'

'There's a brake somewhere?'

'Yes. Take your right foot off the accelerator and move it just a bit to the left, and you can feel the brake pedal.'

Still in first, the car slowed at once. Before Alan had time to mention the clutch, Richie hit the brake and the car stopped abruptly. The engine cut out with the driver still gripping the wheel fiercely.

'You need to be able to release your hold on the wheel with your left hand to change gear.' Alan was still calmly patient. It became easier to imagine him in control of events while under fire. 'Swop places and watch how I do it.'

Richie left the wheel, walked around the car steadying himself with one hand on the bonnet and without a word occupied the front passenger seat. Alan restarted the car and moved away, picked up speed and changed up to third. It was a smooth, practised transition.

'This problem with second gear is a real nuisance, especially for a learner, but you see what I mean?'

Richie remained silent, as though communing with himself.

'And you don't need to keep a tight grip on the wheel. She's got good steering, very responsive. You only want the lightest touch. Look, you can steer with one finger.'

Gwyn and I watched entranced as, with the forefinger of his right hand low on the black perimeter of the wheel, he steered the car slowly down the road's steep camber on to grassy verge and into a tree. With a grinding of metal and a bang the car stopped. The jolt flung us from the back seat in a heap. Not a word was said.

Gwyn struggled up and out of his door. By the time I had gathered myself, he was standing, with Alan, both swaying gently on their heels, looking expressionless at the crumpled right front wing in the glow of the headlights, which had survived intact.

I got out, went to the front passenger side and opened the door. Richie toppled out and fell full length on the grass. I rescued his glasses. He was unconscious or asleep. It took a while to lever him to a sitting position.

'Are you all right? Did you bump your head?'

'Don't think so.' He felt his head and face. 'No – all one piece. What happened?'

'We're not going to the Costa Brava, then?' said Gwyn.

Alan was suddenly sober. 'It's near enough a hundred miles off. Nice idea, but a bit out of our way. I'd better see if I can get the car out of this tree.'

With Gwyn's help he tugged the buckled wing away from the front wheel and in a few moments had restarted the car, reversed and pointed it back to El Masnou. Richie was on his back again, snoring gently, and reluctant to be moved. Gwyn and I dragged and hoisted him into the back, where he slumped. To make room for myself, I held him more or less upright in his seat for the short journey back to the hotel.

Getting him up to the first floor was a problem Alan was pleased to leave to us. It was fortunate customers and staff had gone home or to bed. We thought if he could be persuaded to put his arms over our shoulders we would be able to support him up the rather elegant curving staircase. We propped him against the wall at the foot of the stairs, but before we could organise ourselves he slid to the floor.

'What can we do, he's drunk?' I said.

'Sh!' said Gwyn. 'People sleeping.'

We hoisted him again and he slid down again, saying, 'All right, all right – leave me here for a bit.' At the fourth attempt we hauled him up and got him into position, where he looked from side to side, blinking.

'Richie boy, you're drunk,' I murmured in his ear as he hung between us.

He half-turned his head towards me with a small, sly

smile, as over a shared secret, but couldn't get a word out. 'Mm, Mm,' he said, and remained cheerfully helpless throughout the prolonged struggle up the stairs, his head fallen forward, dark hair hanging down. In his room we allowed him to subside onto his bed, where he lay motionless, fully dressed.

'Goodnight Richie,' we said. A faint smile was our only answer. We left the bedside light on, so that he shouldn't feel totally lost when he came to, closed the door and found our own rooms.

I had drunk only wine and, despite best intentions, having ultimately failed to acquire a taste for it, not overmuch. Besides, I didn't enjoy the lack of control that came with being drunk. On the few occasions when I had taken one too many I usually went off on my own and walked until I felt my head clearing. The curtains in my room were flimsy and I stirred when there was already daylight enough to read by. I had a desert thirst but lay still a while considering my general condition. Having decided I was, in the circumstances, quite well, and hearing sounds of movement on the stairs and in the kitchen below, I decided to get up.

I sat outside where a few tables and attendant chairs had been set out. It was a placid morning, sun still low in the sky, a light breeze coming off the sea and fledgling waves nibbling at the long crescent of sand across the road. An empty ox-drawn cart, the driver half-asleep, rumbled slowly past followed by two panniered donkeys. 'Ah, the traffic in Spain,' I thought to myself, drank a second glass of water poured from the jug I had collected at the kitchen door and dipped into *For Whom the Bell Tolls*, another Hemingway borrowed from the library at home, its orange cover already sun-faded. Two other guests, so far as I was aware the only other guests, had breakfasted together and left. Still no sign of Alan and Gwyn, and not expecting to see Richie, I had my breakfast – coffee, bread-rolls and apricot jam, the same as the previous day, and the day before.

Alan was first to appear, then Gwyn, both pale, squinting in the light and with hardly a word between them. We went inside for the shade. As mid-morning approached we climbed the stairs together to rouse Richie, who was unwell, but putting on a brave face. When he awoke, he said, he wondered why he was fully dressed. He had no recollection of driving the car or being half-carried upstairs and put to bed. He made a pass at breakfast, chewing lengthily and swallowing with reluctance. 'Coffee's good,' he said. We went for a walk along the beach and gradually a semblance of life returned.

'When the lads at home have a heavy Saturday night, they often talk the next day about what happened after they left the pub. There's usually one or two who can't remember much about it, and it's a big laugh to fill in the gaps. I think I've had what they call a blank spell,' he said. 'That's it – I'm giving up drinking.'

'Do you remember dancing with the cook and grabbing her?' Gwyn's question had a hard edge to it.

'Oh, yes, I remember that. I wanted to hold her all night. Such delicious softness and lovely woman-shape, with an earthy, herby perfume about her hair.'

'The kitchen,' said Gwyn.

Dancing with the cook had not been erased, but what happened afterwards remained dim. We described the pantomime of starting the car and the general amusement it caused.

Alan was concerned about the car. When we got back to the hotel the buckled wing was being examined and laughed over by two of the young men from the garage. Together, and impenetrably, in a fragments of a variety of languages (one was certain we four were Polish), helpfully accompanied by gestures and signs, they gave us to understand they could repair the damage.

'How much? *Cuanto cuesta?*' said Alan.

One shrugged disarmingly: '*No, no mucho.* Cigarette?'

I fetched the box of Player's from my room and handed it around. Seeing the greatly reduced contents, Alan and Gwyn declined, but Richie lit up and, inhaling with his usual intensity, began to look almost normal. 'Giving up drinking is one thing,' he said, 'fags is another. I needed this.'

We left the Morris with our new friends and by midday, when it was too hot to be outdoors, we all went back to bed. The sun, risen higher, had passed over the roof of the hotel and our rooms at the front with a view of the sea were no longer flooded with light. I stripped and lay on the bed and thought I might read, but after a few pages I put the book aside and, in spite of the heat, slept.

That evening, at dinner, we drank only water and, with appetites returning, made a good meal of fish with rice and a custard pudding. It had already been decided we would leave in the morning. If the car was ready early, so much the better. To our surprise, it was. In turn we looked and felt where the damage had been. There was barely a sign of it; bulges had been beaten out, the fine curve of the wing restored and repainted.

'Good as new,' said Alan, 'I wouldn't have believed it. You won't get a better job than this at home. Not half so good I suspect.'

We all agreed. '*Cuanto cuesta?*' he said to the young man, who was watching our reaction carefully.

'*Veinte pesetas.*' He held up both hands twice, flicking out the fingers.

'Seven each?' said Alan, turning to us. 'It's a really fine job.'

We were a dozen miles away from El Masnou, skirting Barcelona on another rough road, when Gwyn said, 'Where's our thermometer?'

We all looked along the bonnet. 'It's gone,' said Richie. 'Some bugger's pinched it.'

'Perhaps it was knocked off when we hit the tree.'

'Knocked-off is right, though I'm afraid I can't remember anything about a tree,' said Richie.

Alan stopped the car and we got out and looked. Instead of the distinctive radiator-cap with its indicator needle there was some kind of plug. Closer examination disclosed a large cork.

'Inelegant, but it will do the job of sealing the radiator well enough,' said Alan. 'I think Richie is right, the old Morris has been the victim of a souvenir hunter, perhaps one of the lads at the garage. Shall we go back?'

'No – onwards, to the heart of Spain! Where's that map?'

Alan carefully unfolded it and spread it on the hot bonnet of the car. We were heading west away from Barcelona on the N11, eventually to Madrid. The plan for the day was to reach Zaragoza, about halfway, where we could perhaps find beds for the night, or at least a place to eat, or a market to buy food and save the expense of a lodging house by again sleeping in the car. It seemed a good open-ended plan. No one offered an alternative. But then Alan proposed a small deviation – no more than an hour he said – a side road heading north into the mountains a few miles ahead.

Gwyn looked doubtful. 'Not Llo again.'

'No, not Llo. I think you may have heard of it – Montserrat, one of the famous mountains of Spain, of Europe even.'

'I've heard of it,' said Richie. 'Didn't know we were anywhere near. Didn't think of it, but I know it's associated with St Ignatius Loyola. You can't be RC and not know that. There's a shrine of some sort in the same place. It doesn't mean I'm yearning to go – not the pilgrim sort, I'm afraid.'

'I've read the scenery is spectacular.'

'Just an hour then?'

We all piled in the car. In our experience, outside towns, rough roads were the norm in Spain, and the trail to Montserrat was a prime example. It would have been a challenge to any kind of transport. The Morris shuddered and creaked, lurching from pothole to pothole. No matter how slowly and carefully Alan drove, it was impossible to avoid the obstacles, which seemed to have been deliberately laid to test the most valiant of pilgrims.

He was right about the scenery. We approached the mountain range stretching east to west before us through a zone of ochre and red soil thinly covered with pale grasses backed by the black pine-clad slopes of foothills. The wall of rock we were approaching was greyish in the lower reaches and oddly pink above, where an array of pinnacles stood like the teeth of an enormous saw against the blue sky.

'If it would only stay still,' said Richie, 'I think I could enjoy the view.'

We drove into a square, flat under the blazing sun, with buildings of several storeys at its edges, behind which rose enormous whitish buttresses of rock, like the bulging, bulbous forms the subconscious conjures before you slip into sleep. Small groups of people were standing or moving slowly about the square.

'I think those must be your pilgrims,' said Gwyn.

'Not mine,' said Richie, 'though I wouldn't mind tackling those rock formations.'

We were about to move on when a smartly-dressed man wearing a broad-brimmed hat came up asking if we were English.

'Not really, but close enough,' said Richie.

'I saw your car,' he said, 'and decided you probably were. We're in a bit of trouble: do you know anything about engines? Ours is running unevenly – getting so bad I'm afraid it will stop altogether and then we'll be stuck. And it's quite a long way from civilisation here. I hired the car in the south of France, Cannes – have you heard of it? – near new, from a reputable agent. I expected it to be trouble free.'

I thought from his accent he was American, but in a few minutes we learned he was Canadian. He, his wife and teenage daughter were touring Spain. Alan admitted that, although he was not a mechanic, he had some knowledge.

'I really would appreciate if you'd just have a look at it,' the Canadian said, peering at us from beneath the brim of his hat. 'There's no sign here of a garage where I could get some help.'

We followed him to the car, which was parked around a corner part-sheltered from the sun, a vastly different machine from the Morris.

'I can see it's a Rover,' Alan said, '– new model, too. It should be reliable. Can you open the bonnet and start it for me?'

Even I could tell the rhythm of the engine was ragged and on the verge of stuttering out, little explosions and puffs of smoke were coming from the exhaust, and the scent of petrol hung in the air.

'It looks to me like a carburettor problem. I'll have a go at it, but you really need to get it to a workshop in a town. We've just had a bodywork problem ironed out – very professionally, and cheaply. I think you can trust people here. For one thing, they've had to keep cars on the road – you don't see many new ones about – and that means they take motor mechanics seriously. Is there a toolkit?'

The wife came over, a pretty woman in a long, light summer dress. 'Are you here like us to see the Black Madonna?' she said.

Richie had been gazing at her daughter standing in the denser shade of a nearby alleyway. 'Is there a Black Madonna, too?'

The wife told us about the basilica and the pilgrimage. They were Catholics and visiting the site was one of the reasons for coming to Spain. 'It's certainly worth seeing,' she said.

Alan was apparently dismantling the engine while the husband watched anxiously as each lead was detached, each screw removed. Rather than standing around uselessly, we decided to take her advice.

After the searing heat of the open square, the cool of the basilica wrapped around us a palpable blessing. We followed a little crowd of pilgrims down the nave towards the richly gilded apse, glittering with ornament, and there above the altar was the figure of the Virgin, Christ in her lap, both lustrous black, glowing in the light of tall candles. She carried in her palm a golden orb and beneath a golden crown, her face, a pure elongated oval, wore an expression of benign delicacy. Christ, also crowned, a happy child, looked frankly upon us, his right hand raised in blessing. Some emanation of the faith of thousands of pilgrims over hundreds of years seemed concentrated in those few moments I stood before the altar – for all my church-going, an experience new to me. The pilgrims knelt before the altar, the murmur of their prayers mingling with the hushed voices of others making their way down the nave.

As we were moving away, 'Are you glad we came?' I said to Richie.

'Yes – I suppose so.'

'I think there must be some unique power surrounding a place of veneration for centuries past, as though flakes of belief are distilled from the prayers of countless pilgrims that descend like snow upon each upturned face. You don't see them, but you feel their soft touch.'

Richie smiled. 'A bit over the top?' he said.

It was a crass intrusion on his ground of faith, And, yet, I had been moved by the Madonna and her worshippers, mostly poor and needy, judging by their clothes and the aura of humility about them.

'I thought the basilica, the whole thing, was overdone,' said Gwyn. 'It seemed garish, distracting. How can you keep your thoughts on God in a place like that, all glitter?'

We both knew Gwyn was chapel: he had spoken of attending a *gymnanfa* with his parents when the sound of the old Welsh hymns in the confines of the packed chapel was wonderful, even if you couldn't understand what you were singing.

'I don't see any problem in church ornament,' said Richie. 'Stark puritan Nonconformity, now, is another matter.' And he strode away purposefully, leaving us trailing behind, I assumed to avoid slipping more deeply into dispute with Gwyn.

It was only when we arrived back where the Rover was parked, its engine now running smoothly, that I saw he was talking with the Canadian girl, who was still hugging the shade, leaning towards her, supporting himself with an outstretched arm and hand against the wall, almost above her head. His voice was musical and she was smiling broadly.

Her mother was on her husband's arm near the car,

glancing from time to time towards her daughter, and half-listening to Alan explaining that the carburettor had probably been jarred like everything else by the rough road and the float setting knocked awry.

'Anyway,' he said, 'I've adjusted it and hope it will get you to a garage where, if need be, they can sort it out properly.'

The Canadians were effusive in their gratitude. 'Kate,' the mother called, 'the car's okay again. Come and say thank you. We need to be on our way.'

As she came towards us out of the shade and got into the car, I saw she was, indeed, lovely. 'Goodbye. Thank you again,' the husband said, and they all waved as the car moved away.

Alan was wiping his hands carefully. 'Are you going to see the Madonna?' I said.

'No, I think not. We'd better get back on the road. I'll save it for another occasion.'

Neither Gwyn nor Richie had a word to say as, keeping as best we could out of the sun, we returned to our mobile oven

Richie sat alongside me in the back of the car staring out of the window as the landscape rolled and jolted past. It was bone dry out there, but still patched with green – stands of trees, thickening to dark pinewoods on higher ground and red soil showing through fading grass where flocks of sheep and goats grazed. There was little to see that so held Richie's attention. He was strangely silent and attempts to start conversation quickly foundered on his uncharacteristic moroseness.

Our detour to Montserrat had taken longer than Alan anticipated and he was trying to make up time, beret pulled to a peak shading his eyes, concentrating on the road. He and Gwyn, who held the map, not that it was needed, for the N11, the only half-decent road available, stretched straight ahead, with barely a curve for miles, had little to say to one another. The journey that long afternoon, heading west into the declining sun was unusually quiet. There have to be events, accidents, curiosities to which memory can adhere and, I suppose, little of the sort occurred. One patch of unsurfaced road, hard going for mules and ox carts let alone motor vehicles, is much like another, and we endured a few that day.

Alan glanced at his watch. 'We are not going to make Zaragoza tonight,' he said.

'Lerida is not far off.' Gwyn was checking the map, 'And quite soon after there's a smaller town called ... Fraga.'

He had barely finished speaking when a dark shape began to form on the plain ahead that as we neared took on the definition of a town. It was Lerida. First, an exuberant celebration of green – green crops, tall green trees – announcing a river, then reddish roofs, towers, lancing reflections of early evening light from windows. We entered the town over a fine stone bridge. The same road led us straight towards the centre, which was overlooked by a steep-sided hill crowned with a castle and an imposing church. At the foot of the hill the main street was busy with shops reopening after siesta and progress was slow through public squares among handcarts and the inevitable grey donkeys bearing loads.

The smell of horse and donkey dung mingled with hot cooking oil, herbs and spices wafted through the open windows. We stopped so that Richie and I could go foraging for food while Alan and Gwyn went on in the car to get petrol. Alan took seriously the warning that, outside towns, petrol stations were few and far between.

We bought bread and some apricots and a couple of bottles of cider, then Richie, recovering from his dejection, found a shop where a dozen or more hams hung from hooks in the ceiling rafters. I left him employing mime and eloquent becks and nods to sample and then purchase thinly sliced ham, while I slipped into a newsagents I had seen nearby and bought a small notebook and a pencil. The notebook pages were squared like graph-paper, but I told myself it was just the thing to keep a record of the places we passed through. If I fancied myself a writer, then I'd better start writing. I didn't mention it to Richie who emerged from his shop chewing and holding a packet with a look of triumph. 'First class,' he said, 'best ham I ever tasted.'

The Morris, with a full tank, had returned to the spot where it dropped us earlier, and following road signs to Zaragoza, we made our way out of town. We were soon in open country, downhill for a while before the road levelled out. It could hardly have taken us half an hour before we crossed a canal at the entrance to Fraga. I remember it now bathed in that extraordinary evening light that smooths edges, hides blemishes and makes all green things denser, shapelier, less variegated but somehow more beautiful. We stopped at the lush river bank to have supper while watching the sun set gloriously, down to the merest sliver of intense orange light at the horizon, then a dot only. Stars leapt out of sudden darkness tempting us again to think of lying out under the starlit sky. As we stood considering, a breeze from somewhere made Alan and Gwyn decide against a night in the open. Richie and I took the blankets while they returned to the rexine seats of the car.

We lay on our backs breathing in night air, which was peculiarly perfumed.

'What's that,' I said, '– that sweetish smell? Flowers?'

At home, whenever doing something about our patch of garden was mentioned my mother would be sure to say, 'Why don't you get some night-scented stocks?' and my father would mumble unconvincingly about cabbage, beans and onions. As I recall, he would usually spend time and energy forking in horse manure, of which we had a steady supply, but at that point his enthusiasm for cultivation would evaporate. There was rarely a harvest of any consequence. I wondered whether the perfume that drifted down to us that late evening in Fraga came from the flowers my mother was so keen to have growing in our black, coal-dusty earth.

'Can you smell that?' I said to Richie. He didn't reply.

'Are you all right?' I said. 'You've been quiet – since we left Montserrat. Delayed hangover?'

'No. Just thinking – thinking about that Canadian girl. If I'd had my way, we would have just followed them. I've come all this way and I don't really know where I'm going, or what I want to do with this lovely life. Perhaps it comes with the RC upbringing, my mother worrying what will become of my immortal soul. She would be happy, I know, if I had a call, as they say. Just imagine that – me a priest. We were in the very place today where St Ignatius hung up his sword and dedicated his life to God's service. Me a Jesuit! Oh, she'd really like that – one of God's front-line troops.'

He fell silent and turned as though to sleep, but I was wide awake and intensely curious. 'A Jesuit,' I said, 'like Hopkins?'

'Me – like dear Father Gerard?' he said. 'I doubt it.' And he began reciting quietly, so that I hung on every word, '"How to keep – is there any, any, is there none such nowhere known some, bow or brooch or braid or brace, lace, latch or catch or key to keep back beauty, keep it beauty, beauty, beauty ... from vanishing away?"'

I held my breath as the words came in a cadenced flow, a chain of sounds, one hard upon the next, and then the insistence of it: '– keep it, beauty, beauty, beauty, from vanishing away.' I'd not heard it, or anything like it, before. It raised the hairs at the back of my neck.

'Did you *see* that girl?' said Richie. 'She was lovely. I wanted that beauty now, before it fades, before I deny myself that sensation of fullness inside me – here, where my heart is. You must have felt it, like when you take a deep breath and hold it so that it feels like something wants to burst out of you.'

He was silent again and I didn't know what to say.

'Celibacy's not for me,' he said, 'nothing's surer. He can call as much as He likes.' And then, 'That perfume ... you're right. It's rather sweet and a little musky. Feminine don't you think? Oh dear.'

Above, the stars blazed in deepest darkness. I pulled the rough blanket tighter about me, wrapped myself in it. 'Good night,' I said. 'Good night, sweet Prince ...'

'Enough of that ... good night.'

A gloom not of the night seemed to fall suddenly. I didn't know what to think, except that he had withdrawn a long way and it was useless trying to reach him.

Alan and Gwyn had already stretched the stiffness out of their limbs before Richie and I stirred the next morning. I had taken ages to get to sleep, but then slept well. Richie said he was fine. He looked restored, cheerful again.

In daylight the source of the perfume that hung about the place became clear. We had bivouacked close to a grove of trees festooned with green and purple fruit like small gourds, some projecting almost horizontally from broad-leafed stalks, some hanging like lanterns, and in the grass a scattering of burst fruit. I had not seen before and, as the sun's warmth licked the trees and their fleshy fragrance became heavier, more pervasive, smelled anything like it.

'What is that fruit?'

Richie and Gwyn shook their heads, but Alan knew. 'They're figs.'

Richie was all for raiding the grove. 'I've never tasted a fig,' he said, 'but I've read about them, and it's really rather intriguing.'

Alan thought it unwise to trespass and Gwyn agreed. In the end he satisfied his curiosity by plucking a single dangling fruit from a branch just within reach over the low wall that seemed designed to mark a boundary rather than keep trespassers out. He brought it to show us.

'How do you eat a fig?' he said. 'Do you eat the whole thing? It's quite silky to touch and very soft.'

As he pressed it gently with his thumbs the purple skin split and a fissure exposed the moist, deep red interior. 'Is that what Lawrence means?' he said, almost to himself. He put his lips to the cleft and sucked the sweetness.

'You know his fig poem?'

I shook my head. 'Only *Sons and Lovers*.'

'Look it up. Mmm–you should try this,' he said, and suddenly started back as a wasp landed on his sticky fingers.

It must have taken us three hours to reach Zaragoza, which Alan's map showed was at the confluence of two rivers. The name of the greater I recognised from school geography lessons – the Ebro, but the blue thread on an atlas page did not prepare me for the breadth of the waters we crossed by way of a noble five-arched stone bridge. Almost at once after the bridge the car entered a vast rectangular square enclosed on all sides by tall buildings, including two great churches, the larger with tall slim towers at each corner and domes of glittering tiles.

As I explained, we had avoided stopping in larger Spanish towns. Of Barcelona, for instance, we saw little beyond La Monumental and streets leading to it, but we did spend time enough in Zaragoza to form an impression of a handsome city, lively, too. Perhaps had we stayed longer and seen more that view would have been modified. The point is I have good memories of the place – the blinding heat of the day, shaded arcades with their busy shops, and one curiosity, the sort of thing you cannot forget no matter how hard you try. In the immense glittering space that forms the interior of the basilica, two large bombs were displayed. It took us some time to work out the notice alongside, in Spanish only. They had crashed through the roof during a fascist air-raid and struck the patterned marble floor far below – without exploding. That it was a God-sent miracle of preservation I could believe.

We found a *casa de comidas* in a narrow side-street lined with old buildings of the grander sort, with stout, curved metal grilles protecting all ground floor windows, something between a palace and a prison. The food in the eating house was simple and good and the portions were large. We quenched our thirst with sweet cider. They had good wine, too, we were told, in English, which was a surprise on both counts. Previously in France and Spain we had sampled only the cheapest drink available, which we had no right to expect to be good, and there was little chance of encountering anyone with even a smattering of English in the small towns and villages we had generally kept to. We promised to return and try the wine. A small hotel farther down the alleyway welcomed our custom and gave us a room each and a shared bathroom, luxury again after a night sleeping in the car or under the stars.

When we returned to the humble restaurant in the evening the air outside was redolent of roasting lamb. We were received like old friends:

'You have the best wine with your meal?'

'*Cuanto cuesta?*'

'For you, seven pesetas will buy *vino tinto* of Rioja.' Seeing our blank looks he added, 'Red wine – very good, you see.'

'Two bottles,' said Richie, holding up two fingers, before we had time to debate the matter.

No choice of food was offered; none was needed. We had discs of spicy sausage and thin slices of nutty ham and mellow red wine. This was the best of Spain we agreed, the mingling of cooked meats and wine while the fragrance of lamb baked over the charcoal fire we had seen on entering hung over us.

No other clients entered. Perhaps it was too early, for we had learned Spaniards generally ate late in the evening. Richie ordered another bottle, produced a slim book of poems from his pocket and read aloud to the room 'John Kinsella's Lament for Mrs Mary Moore', though without looking at the page. I didn't know it then but have often read it since, and the last verse comes back as I remember those days in Spain:

'The priests have got a book that says:

But for Adam's sin
Eden's garden would be there
And I there within.
No expectation fails there,
No pleasing habit ends,
No man grows old, no girls grow cold
And friends walk by friends,
Who quarrels over halfpennies

That plucks the trees for bread?
What shall I do for pretty girls
Now my old bawd is dead.

The room was quiet when Richie finished. 'It's an elegy,' he said. 'You can't beat Yeats. Come on Gwyn, you must have learned a poem sometime in school.'

Gwyn looked doubtful. 'Yes – though I'm not sure I can remember one just like that. Our teacher in the scholarship class, back in the elementary school, used to read to us on Friday afternoons, his idea of a bit of culture after a week of tedious exercises in English and arithmetic. Several times he started reading us a story, "John Halifax, Gentleman" – at least I think it was, but anyway he never got very far. A couple of weeks would pass then he'd pick it up and start at the beginning again. In the end we could have recited the first paragraph by heart. It was the same with the poems he read, but that was our fault, because he'd ask us what poem we wanted and we'd say "Sohrab and Rustum, Sir" or "Bishop Hatto, Sir", or whatever, so we pretty well knew those, too. But I couldn't recite them now. In our first year in the secondary school – do you remember? – we all learned "I Wandered Lonely as a Cloud".'

Richie mimed beating him over the head with his book, and then called up from memory passages from 'The Prelude' that I, too, knew but had little regard for at the time. I used to think Wordsworth tedious and much preferred the mysterious imagination of Coleridge, or the dash and swagger of Byron, but Richie's voice that night sounding among the great oak beams of the candle-lit *posada* began to change my mind. He spoke with a sensibility so profound I have never forgotten the northern chill it gave me in the warmth of the Spanish night:

Oh! When I have hung
Above the raven's nest, by knots of grass
And half-inch fissures in the slippery rock
But ill sustain'd, and almost, as it seem'd
Suspended by the blast which blew amain,
Shouldering the naked crag; Oh! At that time,
While on the perilous ridge I hung alone,
With what strange utterance did the loud dry wind
Blow through my ears! The sky seem'd not a sky
Of earth, and with what motion mov'd the clouds!

When he fell silent, I felt a kind of giddiness and thickness in the throat. Gwyn and Alan were quite still and I wondered if they were similarly affected. It was very strange. I don't suppose young men on a continental jaunt today recite poems to one another. I'm not sure it was common then, but there was something about Richie, his way of entering into a poem, and of course, his voice.

If he had then turned to me, I don't know what I would have chosen, and I was relieved when Alan said, 'There's one poem that has stuck in my memory, and I'm not sure why. I used to be keen on Edgar Allen Poe – the stories I mean of course, but in the books I read at that time there were often also poems, and one of them has stayed with me. Do you know "Annabel Lee"?'

We all shook our heads, and he began reciting –

It was many and many a year ago
In a kingdom by the sea,
That a maiden there lived whom you may know
By the name of Annabel Lee;
And this maiden she lived with no other thought
Than to love and be loved by me.

– and so on for a further five stanzas. I think we were mesmerised by it, though the wine of Rioja probably played a part. He had read and re-read it, he said, until with no effort to learn he had learned it. I could understand that, because, as I found later, in my own black mood, it winds itself into your memory like a spell, an incantation. Yet the whole thing was odd, incongruous too, an ex-soldier, hands clasped before him, eyes closed, head raised, that bony, sensitive face in the dim lamplight, reciting a strangely depraved poem, about death and love beyond death, and the living sharing a grave with the dead.

The meal was finished, the wine drunk, the bill paid. 'Let's take a stroll by the river,' I said, and we did. It was an exquisite night, moonlight reflected in the dark water, many couples and families walking the broad footpath along the riverbank, quiet conversation filling the air.

'This is a fine place,' said Gwyn. 'I really could learn to like Spain.'

We all agreed: this was the best of times. For a variety of reasons, we would remember Zaragoza. The sun rose again the next day, and the next, relentlessly, glare and deep shadows lengthening as the hours passed. And mingled with the sudden unwarranted pangs of homesickness that still beset the unseasoned traveller, there was something else, a melancholy sense that if things could not be much better, could they become worse?

It is about two hundred miles from Zaragoza to Madrid. The line of the road was emphasised in parts by trees on either side, not the lofty, swaying poplars of France, more stunted versions, but at least, where they occurred, an edge of green to soothe the eyes. I wrote in my notebook the towns and villages we passed through, and afterwards, last thing at night, I used to recite them to myself, savouring the exotic Spanish names, so that they still cling in my memory, though the notebook was lost long ago. The landscape, too, I remember well, for I had seen nothing like it before. Very clearly I recall, soon after leaving Zaragoza, the N11 rises quite steeply two thousand feet and more, and everything changes with the increased altitude. We had experienced summer heat on the coast, often tempered by a breeze, and on our way inland from Barcelona, but once we were on higher ground, by day it was as though a furnace door had opened, and in the towns, out of the wind, not much better in the darkness of evening.

The first casualty was Richie's butter, for several days undisturbed and unnoticed at the bottom of his case. We became aware of it only when a greasy stain appeared on the exterior. Richie delved for and produced the jar, the butter liquefied inside and, despite rubber rings and clips at the neck, seeping out. The case was packed too tightly for it to have spread through the clothing, but retained its suave touch and buttery aroma after protective paper had been spread over the dark patch inside.

In the long day's travel out of Zaragoza, the breadth and flow of the Ebro were forgotten. The few watercourses we crossed were shallow, sluggish and muddy and we did not meet another clear stream until, days later, we descended the northern edge of the meseta. Calatayud, Medinaceli, Alcolea del Pina, Guadalajara, Alcalà de Henares: what I remember is small towns seen from a distance rising out of the plain, echoing in form and their predominant colour, of dust or pale clay, the mountains rising to right or left. The tall towers and massive stone walls of their castles or convents suggested a significance wildly disproportionate to the number and poverty of inhabitants we saw in the streets. Beyond their walls, often grand walls encircling a property or the lesser walls of animal pens, the soil would be striped red or yellow, but colour stood no chance in the bleaching sun. It was as I imagined the surface of the moon, alien, bleak, and the air above it trembling. When the sun was high you narrowed your eyes to slits to look at the land and all was white, except where rocks sat in black pools of shade. And, later in the afternoon, suddenly at a distance, there would be a curious hill, a *mesa*, flat-topped, its steep flanks striated by winter rains, dark streaks where, as the sun declined shadows gathered, blue, darkening to purple and violet. Sunset came deep red through the dusty haze and the sharp outlines of western mountains were oddly tinged with green.

At one point we stopped to stretch our legs and walked a little way into the vast landscape, with its rim of distant, tortured mountain peaks, their outlines sharp against the sky, and looked back at the Morris. It stood beetle-black on the empty road and, seeing it there, we shared one thought: what a lonely, desolate place.

'I've read the winters here are long and terrible,' Alan said, 'first heavy rains, then bitter cold. All those peaks,' he pointed, 'snow-capped, and a wind to cut you in half.'

'Welcome to Spain!'

'Come on, Rich,' Gwyn said. 'We know it's not all like that.' But cajoling didn't lift his sombre mood.

'There was a lot of fighting across this region in the civil war,' Alan continued, 'as the fascists closed in on Madrid and the poor devils defending it.'

He wore his battlefield experience lightly. Indeed, we would never have known anything about what he had been through, summer and winter, soldiering across northern Europe, if I had not had the temerity to ask. His first thought always was for the endurance and suffering of the ordinary man pressed to fight.

One hour, one day, is much like another where what strikes the eye or ear hardly changes. Returned to the car, we observed at an unmeasurable distance a cloud of dust and, though we moved towards it at the sober Morris's best speed, it was a long time before we heard though the open windows the tinkling of bells rising out of the cloud. At last we passed slowly through the flock of sheep and waved to the shepherds, who saluted us formally, as gentlemen to gentlemen.

After the flock we anticipated a town or village, but none was in sight until a cluster of dust and clay-coloured shapes like scattered shards in a desert emerged in a shallow dip, and in the midst the point of a spire. The road ran through, barely acknowledging its existence, but it had the humblest of taverns. There was no cider and the wine, which we were allowed to taste before purchase, was execrable, but water, fetched from some deep, hidden well was cold and sweet.

'Go on,' they signed to us. 'There will be food. Go on.'

That was how we found ourselves in Alcalà de Henares, looking up at a statue of Cervantes in the main square. We all knew the name. None of us had read a translation of *Don Quixote*, but we were familiar with shortened versions of episodes from it, and the names of characters, the Knight himself and his horse Rocinante, his squire Sancho Panza, his beloved Dulcinea. This we saw was his birthplace, a town of some significance in his day, as vestiges of grandeur in buildings about the square testified. But neither the fame of the writer nor the beauty of the architecture had saved it from a battering in the civil war. The ferocity of the fighting was plain to see fifteen years on in buildings that were shored up and shrouded, undergoing desultory repair, and in the shell and bullet holes pitting fine, ancient structures that had avoided large-scale damage.

On the outskirts of the town we found what might once have been a travellers' inn with an interior courtyard and a gallery surrounding it at first floor level. We drove the Morris into the courtyard shade, among chickens and some goats in a hurdle and two tethered donkeys staring at the ground, motionless, apart from occasional twitches of the coarse grey thatch of their flanks and slow, heavy-lidded blinking. It was the sort of place horse-drawn mail and passenger coaches once called at, a staging post full of life. Now it was much neglected, its gnarled, ancient timbers tinder dry, but the smell of farmyard mingled with hot oil from the kitchen. There was life and a welcome tinged with curiosity.

We shared two rooms where wooden-framed beds had plump mattresses that seemed to have been stuffed with straw, and a primitive bathroom, which we would have shared with other guests had there been any. Was there food we wondered.

'Comida?'

'Si, tenemos comida.'

Late in the evening vegetable soup and a powerful garlic sausage were brought to our table in guttering candle-light. The wine we diluted liberally to take the edge off its vinegar sourness. It was not a poetic occasion and perhaps the meal made for a restless night. Anyway, I stirred at some black, god forsaken hour to hear Richie murmuring. At first I thought he was talking incoherently in his sleep, but I soon became aware of a definite cadence in the sound. He was reciting.

'Are you awake,' I said, speaking softly just in case.

'Awake, yes. Can't get settled. All this rustling beneath me doesn't help.'

'What were you reciting?'

'Anything. Anything really. Whatever comes into my mind. It's what I usually do if I can't sleep – recite something I know very well, that I can run through my mind without thinking. Often enough the rhythm and the sequence of sounds, like a lullaby I suppose, seem to hypnotise me and I drift off mid-stanza. You've done it now though – woken me up properly.'

'Sorry. What were you reciting just then?'

'I've finished the first part of "The Ancient Mariner" – that often does the trick, but not tonight.'

'Wouldn't counting sheep be easier? Still, that piece you read in the bar in Zaragoza is making me think again about Wordsworth. It's the way you tell 'em.'

After a pause in which I wondered whether he had nodded off: 'I've had experiences like that – climbing, when your fingers are straining for grip in a cleft of rock, while your toes inside your boots are searching for a hold, and the wind is buffeting you. You can feel it prising at your hand, trying to pluck you off the rock.'

'This rock climbing – when do you do it? More important, what on earth for? Why do you do it?'

'Nowadays, on occasional weekends. It started a long time ago, before I got to the grammar school, in those quarries on the mountain behind the house. Now it's cliffs on any convenient bit of coast. All very well for Wordsworth, he was born in the Lake District, but I can't afford to travel there. After a while it gets you – a primitive thing. You're right on the edge. You know, really *know*, you're alive. Let go and you're dead.'

After a long pause: 'I've thought about letting go.'

I held my breath, then, 'That's appalling,' I said in a rush.

'No. I don't mean wanting to end it all. Not despair – deepest damned of all the sins, way beyond the deadly seven; though, despite Father Trevor's earnest warnings, I don't understand why. I do think occasionally life is rather tiresome. That doesn't mean I'm "half in love with easeful death". I'm not suffering physically or, for that matter, psychologically. There's no desire "to cease upon the midnight with no pain". But I am curious.'

'Curious? For goodness sake!'

And then I could tell from his voice he was smiling broadly. 'If I'm with Keats, it's when in his mind's eye he watches Madeline as she "loosens her fragrant bodice", and "by degrees her rich attire crept rustling to her knees". We had to study that poem for School Cert. The teacher avoided any mention of those lines, no doubt fearing they would inflame our senses. He was right, too, at least in my case. Yes, "by degrees her rich attire crept rustling to her knees".'

His voice lingered on Keats's words, and then he chuckled to himself, 'Lovely.'

We both lay still; the straw rustling ceased. In the quiet I heard the creaking and cracking of the inn's ancient timbers as they settled to the sudden chill at the heart of night after the heat of the day. Eventually, I suppose, I fell asleep.

Next morning we were glad to rise early and resume our journey. Madrid was barely twenty miles off. At the first street sign announcing the capital we stopped. Even here, on the outskirts of the largest city in Spain, traffic was light. Alan took the snap commemorating the occasion; there is not another vehicle in sight. We got back into the car and drove on.

Having skirted the suburbs, we left Madrid on the N1, signposted Burgos. At the start the road was broad, though the surface little better than well-compressed rubble. 'Fine for military vehicles,' Alan said, and perhaps that was an explanation with the leadership of the country in the hands of the military, suspicious of the motives of their own people.

With rather more than a hundred and fifty miles before us we relaxed as best we could, all windows open and the morning landscape ablaze on either side. Driving was easy, Gwyn said, from his seat behind the wheel, because the road, though often rough, was mostly straight, and empty, apart from occasional slow-moving lorries, and the usual horse- or mule-drawn carts and wagons. There were lengthy periods when it seemed we were the last men left alive, in a small black box trundling insect-like over an empty plain, no sign of habitation, nothing else moving under the sun. But within an hour of leaving the city, the car was toiling up hill and the outlook had changed. Saw-toothed pale mountain ranges appeared to left and right and the land was greener with bushes, and then patches of woodland and, more distant, dark, pine-clad slopes. I leaned over to ask Alan where we were.

He had already carefully unfolded his map. 'We seem to be climbing into the Sierra de Guadarrama,' he said. 'We left Madrid at about two thousand feet, and so far as I can see we are already up over four thousand. You can feel it's cooler.'

We agreed it was, though the sun was still hot enough to bake any part of the Morris it struck, as a negligent hand on the top of the back seat or a window frame at once reminded us.

'The steering wheel is bloody hot,' said Gwyn, holding his right hand out of the window to catch the breeze.

We passed a walled town with the turrets of a castle rising within and the glimpse of a blue lake beyond, like an illustration from a medieval romance, and still we climbed, the mountains edging closer, until we reached a boulder-strewn pass, where we paused to let the engine cool and look about us. It was still, sheltered from the wind, and silent apart from the tinny clunk of ox-bells. Several of the great, long-horned beasts, all wearing hats or curious woolly top-knots for shade from the sun, had been tethered and were grazing on the broader band of scrub the other side of the road.

Gwyn, who had wandered off to relieve himself, came back calling us to see a notice he had stumbled upon. It said we were at the Puerto de Somosierra, 1,640 metres. He shook his head with an expression of wonderment, 'That's close on five thousand feet.'

I remember Richie's comment: 'I've never been so close to heaven.'

It was approaching midday, the sun overhead. We retreated to the shade of grey rocks that Gwyn claimed were granite. A stream tumbling down close to the road filled our kettle and we celebrated with a cup of tea. We breathed the air of the mountain and its scent came to us.

'Where does that smell come from?' said Richie. 'It's rather like human sweat, but aromatic, sweeter perhaps. If you close your eyes – and use your imagination...' He didn't finish.

'It's just the plants.' Gwyn had a flat answer for most things.

Alan glanced up from his map. It's about fifty miles, downhill a bit I hope, to this town, Aranda de Duero, and then another fifty – about, to Burgos. Do you think we might have something to eat at Aranda and look to spend the night at Burgos? OK?'

Was it at Aranda de Duero we ate, more expensively than we expected, fried eggs and goats' cheese and dense white bread, and a jug of wine, which, if we interpreted the patron's words and signs correctly, was of the region. Or was that an experience I recall from elsewhere? I have no faintest recollection of the place, apart from its name, the name I copied into my notebook sometime that day and added to the memorised list I recited to myself as I was falling asleep that night.

When we reached the outskirts of Burgos the sun was going down. Tall buildings cast deep shadows over roads and squares while their upper storeys and spires still glowed and sparkled with reflected light. Evening was advancing, but it was breathlessly hot. We parked the Morris. Its roof, we saw, was filmed with a gilded sheen of dust where a shaft of sunlight travelled over it. Although we were still high on the meseta – there had been no descent since we climbed out of Lerida – the close confines of the city robbed us of the clarity and movement of air on the rolling plain and hills of our day's journey. As soon as we got out of the car we were sweating at every pore.

'I'm parched,' I said. 'Let's get a drink.'

We found a tavern where beer was sold, cold from a deep cellar, and with it came small slices of tortilla in saucers. The rest of the evening is clearer in my memory, much clearer. We went down to the riverside where, as at Zaragoza, a steady trickle of people, families, groups of friends, lovers, no doubt, were strolling the broad footpath. Though voices were not raised, the sounds of conversation rose about them. Further on a band was playing and it wasn't long before we found ourselves, like most others, walking to its rhythms.

'I rather like Spanish bands,' Alan said, '– a change from the military. The one at the bullfight was good of its sort, I'm sure. But all the music seems to have the same character, the same narrow range of moods – dramatic or melancholy, or a strange combination of the two.'

'Our band at home has a big repertoire,' Richie said. 'They could keep you going a whole evening, a whole week – different stuff all the time. Still, I like the music they're playing here. It fits, you know, it fits all this.' He gestured towards the river, the people promenading, the setting sun behind them, the tall buildings across a road filling with bustle – old cars and battered lorries nosing their way among laden donkeys and decorated mule carts.

'The Spanish are great talkers,' said Gwyn. 'What do they find to talk about all the time?'

He was right. Our conversation between friends was sporadic and connected with a small range of shared interests and current events and needs. Perhaps it was because we sensed our friendship, even mine with Richie, couldn't last beyond uni. We were temporary friends skimming the surface of one another's lives, biding our time before real relationships began. True, Alan, though by far the oldest, hadn't settled down. (What had the war to do with that, I wondered.) But Gwyn already had a clear aim and sense of purpose. Richie, for all his quick incisiveness, was fretting and chafing against fate, his God, his faith, his manhood, while I am sure, in 1954, I was in many respects still a child.

We went away from the river into a great public square, far less crowded, and there before us was the cathedral, a magnificent structure, which we would have entered but at that hour found closed. We may well have thought to return in the morning, but we did not.

We found a place to eat and drink a bottle. There was beer again, which pleased Richie. Sometime later, in darkness, walking back towards the car, because we had neglected or been half-hearted about finding rooms for the night, we heard a great clamour from a side-street. Curiosity drew us near to observe a small-scale riot erupting out of a tavern. Men, all men, shouting, yelling, threatening. Blows were being exchanged, bottles and glasses broken. The mayhem threatened to expand, because newcomers were being drawn into the fray. We saw Guardia Civil approaching at a run and quickly moved away.

'What was all that about?' said Gwyn, when we were at a safe distance.

Alan looked serious. 'I don't know, but it could easily be some political issue, harking back to the civil war. A lot of people still hate Franco.'

'There seemed to be two groups, one very shabby and down at heel.'

Richie was right. None of those involved could have been identified as well off, but some, on the receiving end in the main, were distinctly impoverished, like many of the peasants we had observed from time to time on the road.

A little later, we drove through a monumental stone gate and back over the river, looking for a place to park and settle for the night. Close to the edge of town, along the river bank was a squalid, stinking village of huts, which seemed largely made of scraps of wood and hammered-out tin. Dim lights of oil lamps and candles dotted the darkness, and ragged people moved slowly between the low dwellings or to and from the river. A burst of manic laughter made my back-hair rise, but the persistent human voice of the place was composed of groans and complaints and children crying.

'What hell is this?' said Richie, as Gwyn turned and began to walk back to the car.

'I think you'd call it a squatters' camp. There were quite a few across France and Germany at the end of the war, the displaced, dispossessed, mostly pretty hopeless. This is a bit different. I've read about Spanish peasants coming into towns looking for work – or anything to stay alive. Many townspeople have very little to live on, but the peasants have nothing. We may have seen one of the consequences earlier, outside that tavern.'

There was a silent struggle of dim shapes in the foetid darkness and a cry of pain or fear.

'Dear God, it's an image from Goya.' It was only years later I saw the etchings and understood what Alan meant.

'I bet Franco's people are well-clothed and fat.' Richie

said, as we walked to the car, and I heard the bitterness in his voice.

'There's nothing you can do about it.'

We rejoined Gwyn, who had no explanation for his sudden departure from the scene. None of us spoke of the squatters' camp again, but I sensed we were heading for some event, epiphany or climax, as we moved towards our last destination in Spain. Our aim was somewhere on the coast near San Sebastian, where we could relax for a few days before beginning the long trek through France, homewards. We drove a little farther along the road from Burgos and parked on the verge. It was my turn that night to sleep over the steering-wheel.

The road hooked north-east to Vitoria. Gwyn said he recognised the name. As a boy, still in the early years of secondary school, he had become interested in battles where the British had come out on top – it was what had turned him on to history in the first place. Although they were events outside the school course, he read about Trafalgar and Waterloo, and had learned a little about Nelson and Wellington. Vitoria rang a bell.

'I'm pretty sure that's where Wellington's army defeated the French and just about brought an end to Napoleon's ambition to add Spain to his empire. I don't suppose we have time to look at the battlefield?'

Neither Richie nor I expressed an interest and it was as though Alan hadn't heard. Gwyn bit his lip and a slight flush rose to his cheek, but he said nothing and we pressed on. The plan was to reach San Sebastian, about a hundred and twenty miles off, in time to get some lunch there.

About twenty-five miles beyond Vitoria the road turned abruptly north and we began to descend to the coastal plain. We found ourselves in a landscape reminiscent of home, green hills and leafy woods, fields on slopes with haycocks or flourishing, well-watered crops, and small, neat villages, each with a church at the centre. The gloss of grass and trees spoke of rainfall even in summer. The sun was still hot, but the blue sky was moving with the passage of billowing clouds.

The N1, our travelling companion, led us directly to San Sebastian, a fine, big coastal city. But it was early afternoon and shops were closed or closing. We were lucky to find a bar on the long, curving promenade that served us beer and snacks on saucers. Alan suggested we should look for a place to stay farther west along the coast and come back to the city in the evening to see it return to life.

And that was how, within ten miles, we came to Zarauz, with its own long, curving beach, and waves rolling in and smashing white on the brown sand. The pension San Miguel overlooking the shore gave us rooms for three nights, each with a shower cubicle and WC – luxury we hadn't previously met in all of France and Spain. The two oldish women, Ana and Valentina, who seemed to be in sole charge, insisted in carrying our bags and fussed over us as though we were friends or relatives instead of strangers passing through.

San Sebastian was beautiful, we all agreed. It was evening, time for the *paseo*. In a long, rose sunset over the ocean we joined the crowds strolling the promenade, women in their finery and men wearing dark blue berets low on their foreheads, all seemingly content. It was so different from what we had seen at Burgos. Was it the presence of the sea? Had this city entirely escaped the terrors of the war?

'Well, the sea and income from tourists making their way over the border from France may have something to do with it,' Alan said, 'but they didn't escape the war in this part of Spain, far from it.' And he told us that the Basques, implacable opponents of Franco, were the targets of his ally Hitler's slaughter of men, women and children at Guernica, about sixty miles to the west. Hadn't we all seen reproductions of Picasso's painting?

In the narrow streets of the old town on a headland dominated by a castle, we found many cheerful eating places, and hotels and lodging houses of all sorts, but our meal was already booked and our rooms waited for us at Zarauz. Now we all regretted that decision.

'Let's just go and say we've changed our minds?' said Richie.

Fatefully, Gwyn objected. 'Oh, we can't very well pick up our bags and do that,' he said. 'What if they've turned away other people in the meantime? It will be great there, you'll see – a few quiet, relaxing days before we head north. And we've had a good taste of San Sebastian.'

Richie was right, of course. To Ana and Valentina we should have said, 'Sorry, we've changed our minds'. In the end, that's all you can do for the best: say sorry – and mean it – and move on. I wish we'd had the courage to do that, collect our bags and go. I have thought and thought about the moment when, feeling we ought to do the right thing, we silently acquiesced at Gwyn's prompting. We didn't change our plan to stay in Zarauz and that changed our lives, changed everything.

Gwyn was right in one respect. The beach at Zarauz was an enormous stretch of sand between distant wooded headlands, golden in morning light and empty, like the end of the world. There had been a sharp storm in the night. I was dimly aware of it as I slept and the sea was still turbulent when I looked out of the window on huge waves crashing in. A receding tide had left a broad ribbon of foam like dirty soap-suds all along the shore where, earlier in the morning, even bigger waves had thundered. The dark curtain of the storm had been withdrawn with the brightening of day and high, white clouds hurried across a sky of exquisite washed blue.

Richie had been walking before breakfast. He had fared badly in the night from the first stomach upset of the holiday. We three had survived the delicious stew of fish and mussels and other unidentifiable marine creatures the previous evening, and said how sorry we were he had been unlucky. He said he was better, but had no appetite and seemed in low spirits. It was a good day to rest and do nothing. The beach was inviting and by mid-morning we were in shorts or bathers, sitting on the sand, viewing the mystic geography of dark blue and turquoise water in the bay. There was a breeze, like the bustling clouds aftermath of the night squall, and even with the strong sun it felt pleasantly cool.

Richie wanted only to rest, while Alan, Gwyn and I decided on a walk to the nearer headland. He would get himself a tan, he said, to show off to the boys at the Band

Club and he laid his head on folded arms on the skimpy towel and bared his white back and legs to the sun. He was lean, the bony outline of spine and shoulder blades prominent below the circle of red-dark skin at his nape. By the time we returned he had turned over and lay with an arm across his eyes asleep. He stirred as we approached and sat up.

'Could do with a drink,' he said.

The bar of the pension was cool, as was the bottled beer. Richie drank thirstily, saying he was over his stomach problem.

'You seem to have caught the sun,' Gwyn said.

We looked and, indeed, he had. Though dark-haired he had pale skin and after an hour or more in the sun he was bright red and beginning to be uncomfortable. In another half hour he seemed to be radiating the heat his body had absorbed and felt dizzy. He was burning up.

In Zarauz we were close to the border and Alan was able to use his French. Ana who had served our meal the previous evening grasped what he was saying; it was, in any case, enough to see Richie to understand what was needed. She gave us directions to a chemist shop a few streets back from the seafront, where the pharmacist viewed the damage and produced a bottle of chalky mixture with instructions to shake it well and spread it over the burns. Richie said it gave immediate relief, but not lasting.

Stay indoors, advised Alan, while Gwyn and I nodded dumbly. It was clearly the best thing to do, but Richie would have none of it.

'What's the point of coming all this way without having a couple of hours in the sun?'

'Well, keep covered up,' we all advised, 'and put more of that stuff on.'

He sat silent, morose, poking at the sand with stiff fingers. Alan and Gwyn, warned by his example, kept their shirts on and soon Gwyn had buried his feet in the sand fearing they would burn.

I had seen Richie quiet, withdrawn, before and usually talk about books and writers would dispel the mood, but not this time. 'You all right?' I whispered.

'I think it must be like this as you approach the gates of Hell,' he murmured, ' – a burning and blistering of the first layer of skin, just a foretaste of the furnace blast that will go on and on burning, but you're never consumed.'

He paused and I couldn't think what to say. If I'd had a joke, a word of cheer, it might have made a difference.

'I'm counting up all the things I've thought and done that I should have confessed. It's not a pretty balance sheet, and I'm rather afraid it may be too late.'

The whole long curve of the beach was deserted apart from us. We sat or lay there hardly exchanging a word. Alan and Gwyn picked up books and were soon lost in them.

Richie, too, tried to read, but his skin was on fire and he was disconsolate. He took his glasses off and after peering at the sea for a while, 'Bugger this,' he said 'I'm going to have a swim to cool off.'

'Do you think that's wise?' Alan was very dubious.

'I don't bloody care,' he said. 'I can't bear my shirt on

any longer. There's no point in this. I'm going for a swim.'

He stripped, his body bright red streaked with chalky white, ran down the beach and plunged into a breaker, to reappear a few yards farther on swimming more strongly than I had expected, out into the bay.

Why didn't I go into the sea with him? He was miserable: if ever he needed a friend, it was then. Although he was unconscious of the gift, he had given me friendship of a sort I had never experienced before, that opened my mind, gave a perception of values and purpose to my half-formed character. A true friend would have hastened to follow him, tried to lift his spirits, or at very least been a companion to him in his unhappiness. I thought of joining him in the water, but didn't want to get wet, or afterwards feel the sticky sensation of drying salt on the skin. I was comfortable on the sand. I was thinking of my own comfort, God help me, not of him.

It was one of those vile moments of selfishness that you deserve to have haunt you. I have never been free of it.

We watched him for a while before turning to our books. I glanced up once and noticed the dark head bobbing some distance off. The next time I looked up, it had disappeared.

Alan was methodically scanning the sea. 'Do you think he's swum to the rocks?' he said. Gwyn, too, was gazing at the sea and along the beach towards the nearer, eastern headland. 'He'll have a long walk back in the sun if he has. That will do him no good at all.'

'Yes, the headland. He's said how much he enjoys rock climbing.'

It was a nonsensical notion: rock-climbing in swimming trunks and bare feet. Alan looked at me wordlessly and turned away again.

I cannot say how long it was before panic replaced initial unease and growing desperation. After all this time, the least, fleeting reminder of Richie is enough to stir the lurking horror, set it rising from my stomach to my throat, with my heart racing, the pulse thudding in my ears.

We walked down to the sea advancing through the dwindling scarf of foam, Gwyn and I shouting to the air, 'Richie, Richie!'

Back at the pension Ana and Valentina were distraught. With their help nevertheless, Alan contacted the Guardia Civil and shortly two uniformed officers appeared accompanied by a wiry older man, brown-skinned and grizzled, in blue overalls and beret. He was an angler, we were given to understand, who regularly fished from the rocky foreshore of the headlands. He smiled shyly and shook our hands.

Throughout these exchanges, Gwyn and I stood as though dumb, unable to participate in the arrangements and with nothing to say to one another. And we were silent, walking heavy-footed through the sand, as Alan led us to the spot on the beach we had occupied earlier and then towards the nearer headland.

'No, no,' the angler said.

'No, no.' The guardias shook their heads.

We all stood under the sun, a fresh breeze raising the fine sand about our ankles, while the angler spoke carefully and gesticulated with waving arms towards the sea. It was, Alan explained, about the movement of the tide and currents.

'So he might have been swept or pulled the other way from where we were looking.' I was eager to grasp at any hope, but no one else said a word as we turned to the west. In my memory the sea is still rolling in, foam boiling at its edge, sand is grainy between my toes, and the headland is slowly nearing, the details of its shaggy green summit becoming clearer and at the cruel foreshore of jagged rocks bright spray is leaping.

The Spaniards walked together talking quietly, while we trudged silently behind. As we drew nearer the end of the beach, the angler trotted ahead and we saw him clambering into the rocks, disappearing from time to time and struggling into view once more, closer to the flashes of spray. He knew the spot well, the inlets, the deep and shallow pools. The uniformed men joined him and we too searched, for how long I don't know, until with warning shouts we were motioned back: the tide was advancing swiftly. There was no sign, nothing at all. The guardias and the angler came to us with expressions of sorrow. No more could be done.

Back at the pension, as Ana and Valentina approached expectantly, hopefully, we shook our heads, and they covered their faces and hurried away. I had nothing to say to Alan and Gwyn and suddenly could no longer bear to be near them. It was all their fault. If Alan had not suggested a tour of Spain, if Gwyn had said he wanted to spend the summer with Evelyn, Richie and I would not have come all this way. We would be safe at home. Now, as I think again of that dreadful day, I see it was childishly immature to want to lay the blame elsewhere, on others, on Fate, a merciless God. And I remember it was I, with a sudden access of enthusiasm, who had proposed to Richie we should commit ourselves to the trip

I felt my way up the curving staircase to my room like a blind man, clinging to the rail, sank on the narrow bed, turned my face to the wall and wept for my loss, for my sin. Over and over I prayed that somehow he had been swept to land, alive, somewhere up the coast, and he would be tired after the swim, would look for somewhere cool, in the shade, to rest, would sleep perhaps, anyway, wait until the sun had moved off that part of the beach before starting back, and of course, without Spanish it would be difficult to get help to find his way back to Zarauz. It would all take time. He was on his way ... suddenly he would be there again and everything would be wonderful. But I knew then as well as I know now, that he had gone, forever, and the fault was in me; I was to blame, for a failure of friendship, of care, of love.

What Alan and Gwyn had done, were doing, I neither knew nor cared. I stayed where I was, thinking over and over those last moments, Richie's last words before he left us and walked, alone, down the beach towards the sea, sometimes punching the pillow in anger and frustration at my helplessness, or else in a trance of guilt. When I came to myself, shadows had lengthened and merged into deeper gloom. Then I thought about going home without him. What would we tell people? What would we say to our parents, to the college, to Richie's friends? God help us, how could we face his mother?

Early next morning a body washed up a few miles to the west. The guardia civil were informed and the two who had assisted in the search the previous day came to the pension. We met outside on the path overlooking the beach and a calm, sparkling sea. They already knew who it was but a formal identification was required. I thought of Shelley, drowned and fish-eaten, and was sick.

In an abject state Gwyn and I turned to Alan. I would not wish anyone to go through the ghastly experience of battle, but it does breed an essential composure when you face the worst. He told us what had to be done. Then, soberly, he went with the guardias, gave the confirmation they needed and, with their help, sent a telegram. He returned to the pension, where we had sat, silent, waiting, his face a mask. No word was needed, he simply nodded.

A consular official came out from San Sebastian. I sat before him dumbly helpless, useless, and Gwyn not much better, while Alan told him about our journey and, in detail, the circumstances leading up to Richie's disappearance among the waves. He looked doleful, said he was very sorry and would see that the authorities in Spain and at home were properly informed. Learning that we had little of any currency, he said there could probably be an *ex-gratia* payment towards the cost of the funeral. There was no thought then of transporting the body home.

Sometime later in that endless, dreadful day, Alan told us the aged priest at the parish church of Santa Maria had been consoling, especially when he knew Richie was a Catholic. At Zarauz they were used to the drowned, often unidentifiable, washed up during the war and from vessels wrecked in Biscay storms. This unfortunate had a name. Because of what Alan had been able to tell him, Richie would be interred with the rites of the Church. We, his friends, would of course attend?

We looked at one another and I felt the pall of misery became darker, denser. When Gwyn said, 'But we can't afford to stay another two days, or even a day...' the better part of me died. I wanted only for it all to end and to be home. Alan returned to the presbytery. So we left him in the hands of strangers to the mercy of his God.

Throughout the long journey the thought of seeing Richie's mother again in that house close under the mountain's haunch with its dark, monitory print brooding above the kitchen table filled me with dread. What could one say to a widow who had lost her son, her only child? Again I thanked God when Alan, who as commanding officer must have written to the next of kin of men of his company killed in battle, said he would go. And he thereby added the guilt of mean-spirited cowardice to the list of my failures.

Even now, I wake up in a sweat from dreams of peering into blue opacity searching hopelessly for someone. Or some answer. What happened to Richie? He gave no sign he was in trouble. Was he caught in a current, an undertow tugging him down? Was it sudden cramp? Were there cries for help we did not hear? Or did he simply let go?

Earlier that year, during a brief wintry spell when we had just returned to coll. after the Christmas break, it snowed heavily enough to cover roofs, roads and pavements and decorate bushes and trees. Early morning traffic was disrupted but soon reasserted itself on busy routes. Richie and I had a few pints in the evening and late on, with stop-tap looming made tracks towards our respective digs. As usual, we were talking about poetry. Richie was enthusing about Donne, '... an amazing erotic poet, man after my own heart'. Having little beyond bawdy limericks to contribute to the topic, I was content to listen. He was still in full spate, quoting extensively, when we came to the turn where our paths divided.

I didn't want the evening to end. 'I'll walk a bit of the way with you,' I said, and we went on, uphill, where snow lay deeper on the footpath and the going was slippery. Down an uncleared side-road, under a streetlamp, a still figure caught my eye. Another look confirmed it was a snowman. There was no one else about. People were gathered around their fires; here and there dim lights from curtained rooms cast a yellow glow on the snow.

It was about the height of a small man and must have taken children some time to build, but to Richie it presented an irresistible challenge. 'C'mon, let's flatten the bugger,' he said.

He stowed his glasses away and with a run launched himself at the snowman in a flying rugby tackle. I followed suit and a few minutes later we lay, laughing, in a low mound of snow. Richie fumbled in a pocket and produced a quarter-bottle of whisky.

'Medicinal,' he said, unscrewing the cap. 'I bought it while you were in the gents. Have a drink. I think we deserve it.'

I didn't like whisky, but this was one of those occasions you know you want to remember for a lifetime. 'Cheers,' I said.

We took turns. My third gulp of the fiery stuff emptied the bottle. After that, with the heat of the liquor in throat and belly, we went our separate ways.

Richie was always on the edge, one of the quick-thinking sort, one of those who react in the moment. I don't believe it bothered his mind afterwards what he'd done or said. If he looked back at all to that frosty night, tackling a snowman, lying in the snow, sharing a bottle, wouldn't have meant much to him. But it did to me. To me it was an act of fraternal communion. He was the older brother I never had, who could shock and stir me and make me think. You know how it is, the intensity of first relationships with others outside the family. No matter how fleeting, or ultimately meaningless, they are never forgotten. Later I learned cynicism, then my capacity for hero-worship was still intact. What do you call that mixture of regard, affection, esteem (and a little envy) that you sometimes feel, unexpectedly, for another, when you look forward to their company and do not want the evening you have spent together to end? As Montaigne might have said, 'What can you call it, if not love?'

I didn't return to college that September. After the unbearably brilliant white light of Spain, I seemed to go into myself, where there was only 'dark, wearying night'. My mother watched over me, gradually took me (however unwilling) out of myself, nursed my mind. When, with a changed course, I picked up my studies the following year, Alan and Gwyn had graduated and gone on. Alan with the First he'd set his sights on, was doing research at Edinburgh University, while Gwyn, with a modest degree, had somehow found his way into a job in an engineering business in the Midlands, married Evelyn, and settled there. I never saw either of them again.

We had discussed the route back through France two days before. Or rather Alan had told us, pointing at the map spread between the glasses on the table.

'This is the way we came down, from Dieppe: Paris – Orleans – that detour to Bourges, and then mostly on this N20 to Toulouse and over the border – just here – not quite as directly as I originally intended.' He smiled. 'Ah, Llo – you must admit the odd diversion was interesting.'

His finger traced the route and he glanced up to see we were attending. Richie was leaning back in his chair, smoking, looking out at the sea beyond the window. The sun was shining and the sky cloudless blue, but a stiff wind drove waves tumbling one after the other up the deserted beach.

'We're heading north this way – through Biarritz and Bordeaux, and then it's mostly N10,' the finger moved, '– Poitiers – Tours, and then Chartres, and Rouen, back to Dieppe. What do you think of that?'

'Fine, fine,' said Gwyn. 'No – I mean it's a great route. Isn't it Rich?'

'Yes, great.' Richie's gaze was still held by the crashing waves and the blue beyond fading in intensity to the horizon. He drew deeply on the cigarette.

'It's a hell of a long way,' I said, following the moving finger. And, with another of those sudden pangs of homesickness, 'What will it take – three days? Four?'

'If the car keeps going, three days, longish days, to Dieppe and the night ferry.'

An early shower or heavy dew had left the dusty windscreen streaked with salty tears. We had settled the bill after the neglected meal the previous evening, when real tears had flowed, amid incomprehensible expressions of shared grief at which we could only shake our heads disconsolately. With no wish to endure a repetition of the scene, we had packed our belongings, and Richie's books and clothes in his abandoned, grease-stained suitcase, and left the pension, closing doors quietly behind us.

It was a cool, grey dawn, the sky pearled with thin cloud. Alan sat behind the wheel of the car, his fingers holding the choke, while Gwyn swung the starting handle. The engine coughed, started sluggishly and died. No other movement on the road, not even an early donkey-cart heading for the fields, no car apart from the Morris anywhere near. The noise of cranking handle and reluctant engine seemed appalling. We dared not look up lest it had brought Ana and Valentina, who both slept at the hotel, wringing their hands, to the door. At the third attempt the engine fired and Alan coaxed it alive. Without a word, Gwyn and I got into the car, he in the front and I in the back, with the empty seat beside me. As we drew away, I saw the door of the hotel open and a figure dressed in black emerge, one arm raised. Then the car picked up speed, the hotel and the broad beach of Zarauz on the other side began to fall away and I looked straight before me between the heads of my companions through the smeared windscreen to the road ahead.

PARTHIAN Fiction

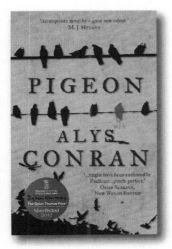

Pigeon

Alys Conran
ISBN 978-1-910901-23-6
£8.99 • Paperback

Winner of Wales Book of the Year
Winner of Rhys Davies Award

'An exquisite novel by a great new talent.' – M.J. Hyland

Ironopolis

Glen James Brown
ISBN 978-1-912681-09-9
£9.99 • Paperback

Shortlisted for the Orwell Prize for Political Fiction

'A triumph' – *The Guardian*

'The most accomplished working-class novel of the last few years.' – *Morning Star*

PARTHIAN Fiction

The Levels

Helen Pendry
ISBN 978-1-912109-40-1
£8.99 • Paperback

'...an important new literary voice.'
– Wales Arts Review

Shattercone

Tristan Hughes
ISBN 978-1-912681-47-1
£8.99 • Paperback

On *Hummingbird*:
'Superbly accomplished... Hughes prose is
startling and luminous' – *Financial Times*

Hello Friend
We Missed You

Richard Owain Roberts
ISBN 978-1-912681-49-5
£9.99 • Paperback

'The Welsh David Foster Wallace'
– Srdjan Srdic

The Blue Tent

Richard Gwyn
ISBN 978-1-912681-28-0
£10 • Paperback

'One of the most satisfying, engrossing and
perfectly realised novels of the year.'
– *The Western Mail*